Dear Reader,

I'm thrilled to be able to share my debut Harlequin Blaze novel with you! I've been a fan of Blaze's supertalented authors for years and am honored to join their ranks with *Command Performance*.

Have you ever wanted to set aside all the things you should do and just do something for yourself? Meet Maggie, a woman whose life is defined by responsibility. But for one night she wants to set everything else aside and go after what she wants—a man who can make her fantasies come true. But what happens when Maggie discovers her one-night stand holds the key to her professional success?

U.S. Army Ranger Hunter Cross loves his job. And he's the perfect man for Maggie's one night of wild sex. He possesses a drool-worthy body and he excels at taking charge, especially in the bedroom. And as their relationship grows, Hunter becomes the one person in Maggie's life who takes care of her for a change.

I loved writing about a woman discovering herself and her needs, some emotional and some sexual. I hope you enjoy Maggie's journey, too.

And I would love to hear from you! Please visit my website, www.sarajanestone.com, where I will be sharing my journey down the road to publication, behind-the-scenes details on the inspiration behind my U.S. Army Rangers and much more. Or find me on Facebook at Sara Jane Stone.

Happy reading!

Sara Jane Stone

Command
Performance

—

Sara Jane Stone

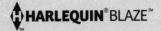

Recycling programs
for this product may
not exist in your area.

ISBN-13: 978-0-373-79774-5

COMMAND PERFORMANCE

HARLEQUIN®

Printed in U.S.A.

www.Harlequin.com

ABOUT THE AUTHOR

After several years on the other side of the publishing industry, Sara Jane Stone bid goodbye to her sales career to pursue her dream—writing romance novels. Armed with a firm belief that dreams do come true, she sat down at her keyboard to write fun, sexy stories like the ones she loved to read. Sara Jane currently resides in Brooklyn, New York, with her very supportive real-life hero, two lively young children and a lazy Burmese cat. Visit her online at www.sarajanestone.com, or become a fan of Sara Jane Stone on Facebook, or follow her on Twitter, @sarajanestone.

To Jill and Brenda,
for making this story shine and for helping me
get it into readers' hands.

To my parents,
who always believed I should be a writer.

To my children,
thank you for napping, and for being
the top two reasons I love having a job
that allows me to stay at home.

To my husband,
for supporting and believing in me.
You're my hero forever and always.

Prologue

"WHERE IS THE CHOCOLATE?" Maggie Barlow stood on her front porch, the door to the three-story mansion that had been in her family for generations open behind her, allowing the cooled air to escape into the hot July night. She watched her best friend since the second grade march up the steps with a pair of four-inch stilettos in her hand. Not a bakery box in sight.

"You need these more." Olivia thrust the shoes at her.

Maggie looked down at the shiny white stilts she held and frowned. Twenty-four hours earlier, she'd caught her supposedly stable and reliable fiancé with his pants down—literally—and his nineteen-year-old research assistant bent over his desk wearing nothing but a pair of pink, fuzzy handcuffs. She needed double-fudge brownies, not shoes.

In a lime-green sundress and pink platform sandals, Olivia looked as if she'd wandered away from a tropical vacation, not the upscale art gallery she managed. She marched into the foyer. "Come with me. I need to look in your closet."

"I ended things with Derrick," Maggie said, following Olivia to the second story. "You thought I was crazy to

marry a man because we had similar careers and interests. You said I was making the safe choice and turning
my back on love because it was too messy. You hated him.
We're supposed to be celebrating."

"Oh, we will, but not here. I have a plan." Olivia led the
way to Maggie's bedroom and pointed to the neatly made
bed. "Sit while I find something for you to wear."

Maggie set the heels on the floor. They were beautiful shoes, but not for her. As a rule, she opted for sensible
flats. She looked up as clothing flew out of her walk-in
closet. Gray and black suits—boring, take-me-seriously
work clothes perfect for a political science professor with
a specialty in military studies—landed in a pile on the
floor as Olivia searched for something she deemed ap-
propriate for her "plan."

"You're lucky there's a car show at the Hudson Val-
ley fairgrounds this weekend." Olivia emerged from the
closet holding the skinny jeans Maggie didn't intend to
wear outside the house until she gave up linguine Alfredo.
Her friend tossed them on the bed and turned back to the
closet. "Put these on while I find you a shirt."

Maggie went over to the growing pile of business suits.
Piece by piece, she picked them up and carefully placed
each one over the back of her armchair. "Why would we
go to a car show?"

Olivia reappeared with a backless green shirt. "The
guys there will love your grandfather's vintage Mercedes."

"The Mercedes is in the shop. I'm renting a Toyota for
the weekend." Her late grandfather's car spent about as
much time in the shop as it did out of it.

"You could afford a new one," Olivia pointed out.

"But I love that car. It reminds me of happier times."
Before she'd lost her mother, before her grandfather passed
away from a heart attack and before her father returned

from war broken, unable to handle the fact that two bullets in the thigh had ended his career with the U.S. Army Rangers. "And why should anyone at a car show care what I'm driving?"

Olivia picked up the clothes she'd selected and held them out to Maggie. "Because we're going to find you a man. I did a Google search for the top ten places to meet men, and 'car show' was in the top five. It outranked baseball games. Now get dressed."

Maggie froze, the clothes in her arms. "I just ended my engagement. I don't need to meet another man. I need to focus on work. I have to face a room full of generals at West Point on Monday morning. They're in town for the president's speech later this week, and the army's demanding I speak with them before they'll grant me access to the team of Rangers I need to interview for my book. This six-man team rode horses belonging to an Afghan warlord to rescue three female aid workers. They're heroes. Modern-day cowboys. If I can secure these interviews, I'll be able to share their accomplishments with the world."

Olivia put her hands on her hips. "You can prepare for your big meeting tomorrow. Tonight we're going out."

Maggie shook her head and set the clothes back on the bed. "Liv, I can't. I have four months to finish this book. My publisher wanted it yesterday. The war is essentially over and my editor is afraid the readers who bought the recent bestseller about the SEALs mission won't care about what happened during the war once all the soldiers are home. If I don't research and write it fast, they'll find another author. They only picked me because I told them I could get access."

"You have a savings account and a home you own free and clear—you don't need to work."

"Thanks to my grandfather," Maggie interrupted. Her

grandfather had been her rock, raising her after her mother passed away while her father was deployed overseas. Her grandfather had been born to wealth and had chosen to serve his country when he could have lived off his savings. In her mind, he'd always been a hero, even though he'd never been recognized for his accomplishments on the battlefield. Unlike her father, who'd received medals and accolades for a military career that had destroyed him.

"But his fortune will run out eventually," Maggie continued. "And it doesn't provide the same stability as a career of my own. This could be my breakout book. Aside from my students and colleagues, no one bought my first one."

"I did," Olivia said. "But you wrote about a bunch of marines sitting around and waiting. It was boring."

"It was an important reconnaissance mission," Maggie said defensively. "That mission, well, never mind about that. If I hit the bestseller lists with my sophomore publication, I'll be a shoo-in for tenure at the college. Tenure is about as close as you can get to a lifetime of job security."

Even her best friend, who'd stood by her through the loss of her grandfather and her father's drinking, couldn't understand. Maggie needed to succeed. If she let her control slip, let one responsibility fall by the wayside, her life would collapse like a series of dominos. She'd watched her father's world crumble when he'd started drinking after his injury, taking hers with it until she'd learned to keep food in the house and the bills paid. But now that her dad had passed away, and she was on her own, she was willing to do whatever it took to keep her own world from falling apart again.

"One night, Maggie. You need to do something for yourself. Something wild. You've been taking care of others for too long. You need to let go. Let someone take care of you and your needs for once. You need a sexual adventure."

Maggie felt her eyes widen. "A sexual adventure? You're suggesting I pick up a man? At a car show?" Common sense told her it was a ridiculous plan, but parts of her body that had no business making decisions tingled and begged her to say yes.

"Exactly. Your greatest excitement shouldn't be a calorie splurge at the bakery." Olivia picked up the clothes and held them out. "Now get dressed. You can't find a one-night stand wearing yoga pants. I'll wait for you downstairs."

Maggie sank onto the bed, her hands clutching the ridiculous shoes. She'd never be able to walk in them, but it was tempting, oh, so tempting to kiss her carefully planned life goodbye for a few hours.

But a one-night stand? When was the last time she'd done that? College. She was twenty-eight years old and the best sex she'd ever had was in college. But even then it hadn't been adventurous or wild.

She closed her eyes. Until yesterday, she'd never have guessed her ex-fiancé would be into on-the-desk sex. And she'd never asked, never said, "that's what *I* want." But no girl who'd spent her high school and college years caring for an alcoholic dad instead of dating would be comfortable saying "this is what I need in bed," would she?

Maggie opened her eyes and reached for the skinny jeans, her hands trembling even as determination welled inside her. Olivia was right. She needed to do something for herself. She was tired of being that girl who was too afraid to ask for what she wanted from a man. Tired of being the caretaker, the writer, the teacher and, worst of all, the dutiful fiancée who got screwed over by her ex. Tonight she was going after what she wanted—one night with a man who could make her sexual fantasies come true.

1

"GOODBYE, CONTROL," MAGGIE muttered, her hands trembling with a mix of excitement and nerves. "Hello, fantasy."

She stepped into the car show refreshment tent and paused, her fingers playing with the clasp on her purse. Fans blasted, but she still feared she might break into a sweat. And wouldn't that be attractive?

She forced her fingers to still. Sexy women, the ones who left men desperate to touch, possessed confidence, not anxiety. If she kept playing with that clasp, her bag might fall open and expose the box of ribbed-for-her-pleasure protection Olivia had given her in the car. Turning red with embarrassment wouldn't help her confidence.

Why shouldn't she feel confident? She was a career-oriented author and professor. And she knew she looked good tonight. She had big breasts and a trim waist—both of which were on display thanks to the backless green shirt Olivia had chosen. Wearing it meant Maggie had been forced to leave her bra at home.

She glanced down at the full D-cups pressing at the front of her shirt as if screaming to the room *look at me!* Had anyone noticed? Had one of these men caught sight of her and said, "Wow! I bet she would look great topless and bent over the hood of my car"? She scanned the tent and spotted a couple of men staring at her, their eyes never drifting above her chest.

"The shirt. It's working," Maggie murmured to her best friend.

Olivia stood half a step behind her, blocking the exit as if she feared Maggie might bolt at any moment. "Of course it is. Now all you have to do is walk to the bar and order a drink."

Maggie nodded, squared her shoulders and wobbled to the bar, silently cursing Olivia for insisting she wear the four-inch heels. Her feet ached for her sensible, everyday flats. But she needed the height advantage. Without the stilettos, all five foot three inches of her would be lost in the sea of towering males.

And there were definitely Men here. Capital *M*. At the tables, on the folding chairs, leaning against the make-shift bar—muscular, don't-mess-with-me Men. The type of guys she'd always admired from a distance, as if they were part of a display with a little sign that read Look, But Don't Touch.

Tonight she wanted to touch.

Some wore uniforms, but most were dressed in civilian clothes. Still, their military-issue haircuts gave them away. They might be wearing jeans and T-shirts, but they were soldiers. Not that this was surprising. It made sense that a car show near a military academy would be overrun with soldiers and cadets. Most men liked cars. The guys in this tent probably spent 50 percent of their free time re-building their engines.

Not Maggie. She'd never even changed a flat tire. Not once.

Her nerves kicked into gear again. Her fingers drummed

against her thighs as she picked her way through the crowd. She fought to quiet them and focus. She was on a mission. And it had nothing to do with car parts and everything to do with hard-bodied males.

When they reached the temporary wooden counter, Maggie signaled the bartender. "Vodka tonic, please."

Olivia raised an eyebrow but didn't say anything before adding a glass of white wine to the order.

Their drinks arrived and Maggie took a long sip from hers. She couldn't remember the last time she'd ordered hard liquor. She rarely drank the stuff, always afraid she might have inherited her father's love of booze, and when she did have a drink, she generally preferred a glass or two of wine, or a beer on a hot summer afternoon. One sip of vodka and she was feeling warm and a little tipsy, which was surprisingly pleasant. It even dulled her desire to drive back down to Manhattan and hurl something at her ex. A few more of these and she might have the guts to follow through with Olivia's crazy plan.

"Liv, you do realize most of these guys are soldiers. Probably half either teach at or attend West Point." Maggie noticed she'd downed half her drink. "What if I end up having to deal with one of them while researching my book?"

"Relax, you won't." Olivia shook her head. "Anyway, I thought the men you were interviewing were based in Tennessee."

"They are, but the generals are in town."

Olivia reached over and patted her hand. "I promise I'll make sure he's not a general."

"But I could never date a soldier."

"It's only for one night," Olivia reminded her. "Why should you care what he does for a living if you're not planning on seeing him beyond tonight? Maybe you'll get lucky and find a mechanic. This is a car show."

Maggie drained the rest of her drink. "What if I pick a guy and he turns me down?" Her nerves—and the vodka—sent her stomach into somersaults. "What if I make a complete fool of myself? It's not like I have a lot of experience with men."

"Look at me." Olivia leaned closer. "You can do this. Now. Tonight. If you don't, then duty, responsibility, your need to be the best at your job—it will smother you."

Maggie held on to the bar with one hand as Olivia's words sank in. Her sense of duty had started smothering her years ago when her father began drinking. This was her chance to escape. If she didn't act now, she might lose the part of herself that craved orgasms. The part of herself that wished she'd told her fiancé she wanted wild sex on his desk and so much more.

"You're right," Maggie said softly.

Olivia smiled and signaled the bartender for a second round. "Now, look around. See anything you like?"

Feeling the vodka pulsing through her, Maggie boldly scanned the refreshment tent. What was she looking for? Muscles. The kind that came from the hard work required to transform a man into a soldier or from lifting engine parts. But four out of five guys in here looked like they could bench-press her one-handed. And thanks to her breasts, she wasn't one of those hundred-pounds-soaking-wet women.

She took a second look and mentally eliminated about half of them. Too young. She wanted a man who knew things about sex. She wanted an orgasm that left her breathless, boneless and begging for more.

Her gaze landed on a green polo, tight but not too tight. And those biceps? They shouted *touch me.* Her eyes drifted over his shoulders to his face, framed by straight brown hair. She'd always liked brown hair. Staring at his profile—he was deep in conversation with an equally handsome but not quite as sexy man across the table—she could see his mouth curving upward in a half smile. Those lips. He had the type of mouth that begged a woman to say *kiss me lower down, please.*

Maggie clutched her drink and drew her gaze away from his face. Twelve months of unfulfilling sex had driven her mad if she was thinking about his lips kissing her *there* before she'd even said a word to the guy. She blinked and took in the rest of him. She could see the endless length of his legs stretched out beneath the table.

Her body tingled as she drank in the sight of him. With a long, sculpted body like that he must know how to do things, deliciously sinful, wild things that previously only existed in her fantasies. He turned and looked right at her, and then smiled. She tightened her grip on her nearly empty drink. *Those eyes. That mouth.* She'd bet her inheritance that man knew ten ways to give a woman the best orgasm of her life. If he looked at her like that much longer, she might come right here. Her thighs tightened at the thought. This man would say yes. He wouldn't turn her down. Not after that look.

Maggie blinked and turned to the bartender. "Cancel the vodka tonic. Just water, please."

The liquor had made her bold, maybe even a little reckless, but if she wished to remember every detail about tonight, she needed water. "Do you remember George Clooney when he was young? When he was on *ER?*"

"Oh, yeah." Olivia took her wine from the bartender. "He was on the show when we first started watching it in high school."

"Green polo, blue jeans at eight o'clock."

Olivia raised an eyebrow. "He's not your usual type."

"He has George Clooney's eyes. Bedroom eyes." Maggie reached for her water and drained half the glass. "Tonight, he's my type."

2

CHIEF WARRANT OFFICER Hunter Cross knew a come-on look when he saw one. A look that said, *I want you naked in my bed. Tonight.*

He leaned back on his rickety wooden folding chair and let a slow smile spread across his face, a move he'd perfected at sixteen to get the captain of the debate team into the backseat of his mother's car. He'd always had a thing for supersmart girls. Of course, he'd moved beyond sex in the backseat since high school, but not much. *Commitment* was a dirty word in his mind, and *long-term* made him shudder. Not even the woman at the bar with her soft shoulder-length curls or touch-me breasts would tempt him to change his mind.

Across the room, the blonde pursed her lips, unsure if she should proceed with their unspoken dance. That expression. It was a mix of bold and innocent, an intoxicating combination that went right to his crotch. He let his eyelids lower slightly.

"I know that look isn't for me," Riley, his friend and former team leader, said from across the table.

"The blonde at the bar. She just gave me a green light."

Riley chuckled. "You've been in town for less than three hours and you've already found a woman."

"Hey, I've been laid up in a hospital for two months." Before that, he'd been in Afghanistan. He would have left unscathed if his team hadn't been ordered to rescue three female aid workers traveling to a remote clinic. And thanks to a teammate's mistake, he'd taken a bullet in the process.

"How's your arm?" Riley asked, his expression serious.

"Fine." Hunter rolled his shoulder. It still ached. Nothing the blonde couldn't fix.

"Logan feels awful about how it all went down."

Hunter started to say it wasn't Logan's fault, but stopped. They both knew it was. His friend and teammate had been distracted after losing his young wife to cancer before they shipped out, and as a result he'd messed up—and Hunter had been shot.

"Any thoughts about getting out? Resigning your commission?" Riley asked.

"Hell, no."

"I heard one of those private security companies offered you a job," Riley said quietly.

"Yeah, but you know me. I live for being a Ranger. Hell, I'm hoping they'll give me your old job." With Riley bowing out as head of their team, Hunter was in line for the job he'd always dreamed of and a pay hike. A small one. "I could sure use the extra cash."

"Trust me, the pay bump is so small you'll barely notice. It's nothing compared to what those private companies pay." Riley pulled out his wallet. "But I can help you out tonight. The beers are on me. I need to be getting home."

"Curfew?"

"I like to be in bed with my wife before she falls asleep,"

Riley replied with a smile. "If you ever settle down, you'll understand."

"I think I'd take another bullet before relinquishing my freedom."

"Someday you're going to eat those words. When the right woman comes along, you're going to fall so hard you'll give up everything to be with her. Everything."

"Did they brainwash you when you made those vows?" Hunter joked. Riley didn't know he'd already sacrificed everything he had for his sister. He had nothing left to provide for a wife and family of his own.

Riley laughed.

"Listen, I think it's great what you've got," Hunter said. "But I'm committed to the army. I'm dying to get back to active duty. Married life? It's not for me."

"If you say so." Riley set a twenty on the table and stood. "Think you can catch a cab back to the hotel if things don't work out with your green-light girl?"

That's no girl, Hunter thought. *She has "woman with needs" written all over her.* "Don't worry about me. I'll find my way to bed."

Riley slipped his wallet into his back pocket. "If you end up sticking around the area for a while, give me a call and I'll drive down for another drink."

"Will do. But next time I pick the venue. Not that I didn't enjoy picking out replacement parts for your wife's truck."

Riley patted him on the shoulder, his good one. "Deal."

Hunter's gaze shifted to the cash on the table as his friend headed toward the exit. In the past, he'd have insisted on paying for his own beer. But right now, his cash flow situation was pretty dismal. If he hadn't been ordered to fly up here when he'd been released from the physical therapy center, he would be crashing on one of his team-mates' couches until they were deployed again. With his sister back in rehab and all the bills coming to him, he could barely afford the beer in his hand.

Hunter took a long sip. In his book, family came first. Always. His sister was the only family he had left. He refused to lose her to a meth overdose.

"Mind if I join you?"

The soft words yanked Hunter away from his thoughts. The woman from the bar stood with one hand on the chair next to his, her blue eyes wide and uncertain. Her other hand maintained a death grip on her glass. Nerves, he guessed. She might be playing the part of the brazen blonde tonight, but he'd bet his next paycheck that casting come-hither looks at strangers wasn't a habit.

Hunter smiled and stood to pull a chair out for her. "Please." He extended his hand. "Hunter Cross. And you are?"

"Maggie." She shook his hand and then slipped into the chair. He'd noticed the smooth expanse of skin exposed by her backless shirt when she'd been at the bar, but seeing her up close made him want to touch, to run his hand over the place where her bra line should be, but wasn't. He moved back to his chair to admire the view from the front. Little Miss Maggie's taut nipples strained against the thin fabric.

God help him, he loved breasts. And full braless breasts? They drove him wild.

The woman who now stood beside him looked as if she'd gotten lost on her way home from a cruise ship. "Three questions and then I'll leave you two alone."

Little Miss Maggie's friend had rushed over to "help."

Great. But he didn't try to send her back to her ship. He merely nodded, prepared to face the interrogation. "Okay."

"Are you married?" she demanded.

"Fair question." He didn't take his eyes off her face. He could understand a friend looking out for her own. "No, ma'am."

"Are you a soldier?"

Hunter hesitated. He knew lots of women picked up soldiers. As a rule, he tried to steer clear of them. Women on the hunt for a hero wanted commitment no matter how much they pretended otherwise. Marriage might be perfect for Riley, but the last thing Hunter needed was another person to support.

He glanced at Maggie. The brazen blonde who'd approached him sat biting her lower lip, her brow furrowed as if she was trying to decide whether she should punch her friend or turn tail and run. He lowered his gaze to her chest. Hunter wanted her to stay. Badly.

"Yes, ma'am." He met the friend's challenging gaze. "Army."

His interrogator frowned and turned to Miss Maggie. "He's not a mechanic."

A mechanic? Seriously? He'd never heard of women trying to pick up mechanics. Maybe New York ladies were more practical. Why snag a soldier when you could have someone around to fix your car?

But he couldn't let Miss Maggie walk away because he didn't take apart engines for a living. He smiled. "I'm not. But I know how to change a tire."

"Great," Maggie said, her brow relaxing.

"Are you a general?" her friend demanded.

He let out a bark of laughter. A general? What the hell?

Sure, some women went after navy SEALs. Maybe some even wanted army rangers. But autoworkers and generals?

"No, ma'am."

Maggie's friend gave him a long, hard look as if she thought he might be lying, and then to his surprise nodded. "Good." She looked down at Maggie. "I'll take a cab home. Call me tomorrow." She waved as she walked toward the exit, blinding everyone in the tent as the light caught her shockingly pink shoes.

Hunter shook his head and reclaimed his chair. "What do you have against generals?"

"They intimidate me."

"But I don't?"

She smiled and leaned toward him. "Oh, no, you do. But for other reasons."

"Such as?" If she was looking to secure a soldier, she was sure going about it differently. Most ladies asked a few questions about his latest trip overseas and then declared him *"sooo brave,"* at which point Hunter walked away.

Nothing but a direct order could drag him away from Maggie.

"Reason number one, I haven't done this before." She waved her free hand through the air. The other hand remained glued to her glass. "Pick up someone. A man. At a car show refreshment tent."

He nodded. Bold with a serious case of nerves. And she'd chosen him for her first time. Why? he wondered. His eyes dropped south. They'd get back to the whys. Right now, he wanted to get her naked. But first she had a list of reasons. Hunter grinned. Little Miss Maggie was both beautiful and amusing. For a woman like her, he could afford a little patience. "And reason number two?"

She pursed her full lips, drawing his gaze to her mouth.

The sight of her nipples had attracted his interest, but her mouth? The thought of those pink lips touching him went straight to his groin. Hunter reached for his pint glass.

"I'm trying to decide what I need to know about you before we end up in bed together."

He coughed and sputtered, nearly covering the front of her shirt with the remains of his beer. Once he'd regained his composure somewhat—his dick was harder than ever—he pushed back from the table. "You think about that and I'll get us another round. What are you drinking?"

"Water."

Hunter sidled up to the bar, ordered two waters and paid for the earlier beers with Riley's cash. He'd found the perfect woman, or rather she'd found him—easy on the budget and eager to jump into bed with him. He'd met more women than he could count who swore up and down they did not want a relationship, but brazen-yet-sometimes-shy Maggie was the first he suspected who might mean exactly what she said.

The bartender placed two glasses and a stack of singles in front of him. Hunter took the hint and left a big tip. It was easy to be generous with Riley's cash. Once he got Sierra out of rehab and employed—God help him—he could afford to drop large tips with his own money. Pushing the less-than-pleasant thoughts away, he went back to the table.

"Your water, Miss Maggie." He slid the glass in front of her.

The corner of her mouth turned up. "Thank you."

He picked up his chair and flipped it around. Straddling the seat, his arms resting on the low wooden back, he asked, "So, what would you like to know?"

She stared down at the table a moment then asked, "Do you live around here, or are you just visiting?"

He'd never had the luxury of honestly and openly interrogating the women he met, but if he'd been in her shoes he would have asked the same thing. His gaze ran down her jeans-clad legs—not long, but a good fit for her height—and landed on her lofty heels. Okay, so bacon might sprout wings before he'd wear those supersexy shiny white things, but it was still a good question. "Just visiting. A work thing next week."

A hint of a smile flashed across her face and her stick-straight posture eased. Relief, he guessed. He waited for her to ask him where he was from, how long he'd been in the army or what exactly he did, which he couldn't tell her, but Miss Maggie didn't say a word. "Anything else?"

She drew a deep breath and stared at her water. For a fleeting second, he wondered if he'd read her wrong. He couldn't tell if she was gathering up the courage to ask another question or run away.

Just when he thought she might ditch her heels and sprint to the exit, she looked him straight in the eye. "No more questions."

How close is your bed? He kept his mouth shut, waiting for a better response to pop into his brain. Problem was, his brain wasn't doing the thinking anymore.

"But," she continued.

God help him, there was a but. He reached for his water and brought the glass to his lips, hoping it would take the edge off the get-her-naked-now feeling pulsing through him.

"I need to make sure we're on the same page here." She looked him straight in the eyes, as if she were about to reveal weapon launch codes. "I want an amazing orgasm. Actually, scratch that. I want more than one. So if you don't think you can deliver, or if you're looking for more than one night, I'll thank you for the drink and leave. Because I really need those orgasms."

He could have sworn he was dreaming. In his wildest fantasies, he'd never imagined he'd meet someone like her. A woman who demanded orgasms, lots of them, without commitment.

Could he deliver? Hunter set the nearly empty glass back on the table. "Honey, I'm your man."

3

THE PLAN HAD WORKED. Hunter Cross, the man with the bedroom eyes, was looking at her as if he couldn't wait to tear her clothes off. She could tell from the tension in his body that he was ready to jump up from the table. He'd just drenched the front of his clothes and he didn't seem to give a damn. That's what she wanted, a man who cared more about her pleasure than his own comfort.

A rush of excitement washed over her, leaving her skin tingling, waiting to be touched. The feeling took her by surprise. It had been so long since she'd felt that first spark that she barely recognized it. *This is what I've been looking for,* she thought.

"But first, I have a few things I need to know about you before I get into bed with you," he said calmly.

Or maybe not. He didn't sound like a man blinded by lust. Maybe she was so desperate for a wild night in bed with a man who made her breasts ache to be touched that she'd imagined his interest.

Her stomach flipped and she reached for her drink, needing to hold something. Why had she picked the most handsome man in the tent, maybe in the entire state of New York, for her conquest? And why hadn't she started with a normal conversation? She could have asked him what he did in the army, or where he was from. Instead, she'd demanded an orgasm.

Her finger traced the rim of her water glass. Maybe she should run away now and spare herself any further embarrassment. She could stop on her way home and buy a vibrator. Throw in a cinnamon bun and that might be all the wild and crazy she needed in her life right now.

Except her fantasies didn't involve batteries.

"What would you like to know?" She tried to sound casual, which was hard given she'd whispered the words.

"Do you live around here?"

She looked up at him and felt her building sense of oh-God-what-have-I-done fade away. His George Clooney eyes said *I want you,* while the laugh lines around his mouth indicated he wanted to play a bit first.

She couldn't feel the vodka anymore, but her sense of daring, the one that had driven her to wear the skinny jeans even though she'd sworn she'd wait until she lost a few pounds, returned. She leaned forward, watching his gaze fall to her chest. "Yes. About twenty minutes away."

"Favorite color?" His eyes never left her breasts.

Maggie set her water on the table and leaned back, clasping her hands behind her chair as she pretended to consider his question. Her cotton shirt pulled tight against her nipples and she swore she heard him mumble a curse. "Green."

"Favorite food?" he asked, his voice low.

"Linguine Alfredo." Most of which went straight to her thighs. But she didn't give a damn about that right now. All she cared about was his eyes on her chest and the warm rush it sent down her body. If he didn't hurry up with his questions, she might explode right now before he even touched her.

He drew his dreamy gaze up to her face. His eyes locked with hers. "Where do you like to be kissed?"

"Everywhere," she whispered.

"Be specific," he demanded.

"The back of my neck."

He nodded. "A good place to start."

The nerves on her neck tingled in anticipation, and lower down her body ached. How had he pushed her so close to the edge of an orgasm without even making contact?

"One last question."

She nodded.

"Do you like…"

He paused and Maggie leaned toward him, drawn by the unbelievably sexy sound of his voice.

"Nachos?" he asked.

Maggie blinked, falling back in her chair.

"You know, chips drowning in fake cheese?" He smiled. "I thought we might go for a walk around the grounds before we started working on your orgasms. I remember seeing a nacho stand near the picnic tables."

Oh, you've already started working. Her body hummed with anticipation. Between his eyes, his body and his enticing voice, this man could probably seduce just about any woman. Talk about finding a one-night stand with experience.

"Sure," she said.

"Great. I like a girl who isn't afraid to eat fake cheese." Hunter pushed himself out of the chair in one fluid move. He reached for her hand and drew her up. Wobbling on her heels, Maggie held on tight when he began to release her. She curled her fingers around his much larger ones, enjoying the feel of his strong grip. Her own hand seemed delicate by comparison. So what if he was a soldier? If the old saying about a man's hands offered any indication of what waited for her in his pants, this man's equipment would deliver.

He led her through the exit into the hot, summer night. The sound of voices, mostly male, and engine parts filled the air, both men and parts still visible in the bright evening sunlight. Seven o'clock, give or take a few minutes, in the evening on a July night in upstate New York. It would stay light until nine—perfect for a car show, but not so great for her courage.

Away from the dimly lit tent, reality came crashing down. What was she doing wandering off with a virtual stranger? What if he was some kind of psychopath? He'd admitted he was a soldier and Maggie knew from personal experience that some of the men who returned from war zones had...problems.

She pulled free from his grasp, pretending she needed both hands to shield her eyes from the sun.

"I left my sunglasses in the car," she mumbled.

Hunter nodded and hooked his thumbs through the belt loops on his jeans. "The nacho stand is just beyond the hubcaps."

Nachos. They weren't hopping into bed yet, just grabbing a bite to eat. If he turned out to be crazy, she could ditch him and race back to her car. Not that she'd be able to figure out if he was an ax murderer over chips, but she could ask a few more questions.

Falling into step beside him, she said, "So what do you do in the army?"

"Honestly—" he looked down at her with an apologetic half smile "—I can't tell you much."

"Top secret missions?"

"Something like that." He led her up to a red-and-white stand with signs for hot dogs, nachos and cotton candy.

"I'm a Ranger, part of the Special Forces, and our missions are classified. My teammates can't even tell their wives and girlfriends, not that many of the guys are married, about what we do and where we go."

A Ranger. Like her father. Like the men in Tennessee she planned to interview for her book. Maggie froze, every muscle in her body tensing. The tingling feeling in her breasts? It vanished.

She took a step back and then stopped. The part of her that craved an orgasm from a toned man with big hands and bedroom eyes told her to stay. For the first time in as long as she could recall, the need for an orgasm, the desire to shove her responsibility aside for twelve blissful hours trumped the warning bells.

"What can I get you?" the man behind the counter asked.

Hunter stepped up and Maggie followed. This wasn't about forever. She could pretend he was an ordinary foot soldier if she wanted. The fact he was a Ranger wouldn't matter in the morning and it certainly wouldn't change anything once they took off their clothes.

"Nachos," Hunter replied. "Extra cheese."

"So you came for the food?" she asked lightly, turning the conversation away from his military career.

Hunter accepted a to-go container piled high with cheese-covered chips, paid the vendor and led her to an empty picnic table. "Nope, the food is a bonus. My buddy needed to pick up a few parts for his wife's pickup."

"Not into trading car parts?" She slid onto the bench.

"My truck could use a tune-up, but I'm not the man for the job. What I said before about changing a tire? That's about the extent of my mechanic skills."

"Well, you're a step ahead of me. Every time I get a flat,

I have to call for help." She reached for a chip to keep her nervous hands busy.

"Is that why you were looking for a mechanic tonight?" he asked. "Need someone to call next time you have a blowout on the highway?"

Underneath the table, his leg brushed up against hers. He moved away, suggesting the touch had been an accident, but Maggie felt a rush of heat just the same, running up her calf past her thigh to her core. If he left her this turned on with an accidental touch, what would happen when he ran his palms over her bare skin? Her gaze fell to his large, capable hands, moving up his forearms to where his biceps disappeared beneath his shirt. In her imagination, his shirt vanished, allowing her to feast on his chest, over his sculpted abs and lower...

Her nipples peaked harder at the mental picture.

"Nope. You're just what I was looking for," she said. Was it her imagination or did her voice sound sultry? Maybe even a little seductive? All from one brush of his leg.

"I think that's supposed to be my line," he said, looking her straight in the eyes now. He'd been staring at her breasts and they both knew it. Was he mentally undressing her? Picturing what lay beneath her green shirt? Maggie shifted on the bench, her body desperate to move, to touch and be touched. Across the table, Hunter held her gaze the way a soon-to-be lover would—with intent.

Maggie stared back, noting the golden flecks in the rich brown of his eyes. Her lips parted as if they had an inkling of what he wanted to do. Would he kiss her? Tear off her clothes and take her right here, right now, bending her over the picnic table?

She blinked and looked away, the image too hot to handle over nachos. Was she ready to move beyond chitchat and accidental touches? The new Maggie cried *yes,* but not here. Not yet. One kiss from this man would lead somewhere, and she didn't want their first round to be in the backseat of a Toyota at the fairgrounds. Definitely not part of her fantasy.

"So you're Special Forces and all you can do is change a tire?" she asked, trying to shift the mood before she reconsidered her position on backseat sex.

"You didn't hear this from me, but over the years I might have learned how to hot-wire a car." He used one chip to scoop up a pile of loose cheese. She followed the movement of his hand to his mouth. How would those lips feel against her skin, trailing kisses up her inner thighs, lingering over the place that was pushing her closer and closer to saying *forget the chips and take me to bed, right now?*

Not yet, she reminded herself. Forcing aside the image of hot kisses, Maggie pointed to a table full of knobs and pipes. "But you couldn't tell me what those are?"

He finished chewing and raised an eyebrow. "Do you really want to talk about car parts?"

His leg pressed up against hers, and this time it stayed there. Definitely not an accident. It was as if he couldn't sit across from her and not touch her. It should have made her nervous, the clear, physical signal that this man wanted her. But it didn't. Instead, excitement and anticipation flooded her body to the point where she could barely remember what they'd been talking about.

Car parts. He'd asked if she wanted to discuss car parts. The answer was no. But—

"What do you suggest?" she asked.

"Now that we've eaten, I'm ready to start thinking about those orgasms you asked for. Unless you need more time. We can take a walk around and peruse the merchandise. But I had to say something. It was starting to feel like the elephant at the table. I keep trying for small talk, but the O word is front and center in my mind."

"That's my fault." She clasped her hands together on the table. "I'm bad at this, and I should never have been so direct."

"Hey, I liked your approach." Hunter reached out and rested one of his large hands on top of hers. It was an intimate gesture, but it felt right. More than right, it felt good. Reassuring. "It was a first for me, but a welcome break from most boring getting-to-know-you conversations."

"So you've had a lot of experience with this? With one-night stands?"

"A time or two." He shrugged. "I'm one of those guys who run away from romantic commitment. But orgasms? Those I can deliver. But first…"

His voice trailed off as he rose slightly, reaching across the table with his free hand.

"What?" she asked.

"You have some cheese on your cheek."

Cupping her jaw in the palm of his hand, he swept his thumb over her face, gently brushing the corner of her lips. Maggie hadn't learned much about men growing up, but she recognized the soft stroke against her skin for what it was. It had nothing to do with fake cheese. This man wanted to claim her.

He returned for a second sweep, this time running over the full width of her lips. She leaned into his touch, relishing the warm sensation between her legs. She parted her lips and allowed her tongue to dart out and lick the cheese off his hand. Then, in a move the old Maggie would never have considered, she captured his thumb between her lips and gently drew it into her mouth, sucking lightly. His smile widened, suggesting he liked her bold response to his simple touch. She ran her tongue up and down his thumb the way she longed to lick another part of his anatomy.

Hunter let out a low moan. No doubt he'd understood her unspoken message loud and clear. She didn't want to be the only one enjoying orgasms tonight.

"Maggie." He spoke softly, barely above a whisper, his eyes locked with hers.

That one word, her name, made the sizzling heat between them jump from an I-think-I-want-you eight to an I-must-have-you eleven. Forget sex in the backseat of her car. If one of them didn't pull away soon, they might be heading toward sex on the picnic table after all.

Smiling, he withdrew his hand. Maggie felt the absence from head to toe, but silently promised herself it wouldn't last long. Once they were alone, she had every intention of running her lips over him again. And she wouldn't limit herself to his thumb.

"So, what will it be?" he asked, his tone low and seductive.

"Car parts or orgasms?" She tucked a curl behind her ear. "Orgasms, please."

"I have one more question." Hunter stood and walked around the table to offer his hand. He'd recovered his light, playful tone, but his gaze remained intent. "Did you drive here?"

Maggie placed her hand in his. "My car's parked in the lot."

"Great. My hotel is five minutes from here. Unless you'd rather go to your place?"

"No, we can't go there." On her feet and steady, she pulled her hand free and turned to pick up her purse, hoping he hadn't seen the panicked expression flash across her face. She couldn't take him home with her. She needed the freedom to walk away in the morning, or tonight, if things didn't go as planned.

"Marriott it is," he said playfully. Maggie felt her panic ease. "May I have your keys?"

She led the way to her rented Toyota, rummaging through her bag. She'd gone for sexy shoes, but opted to keep her sensible holds-everything-but-the-sun purse. Including the condoms Olivia had given her. She stumbled as her hand brushed the box.

"Easy." He took her elbow and guided her through the crowd. Maggie kept her eyes on the exit gate. She felt her face flush and knew if she looked at him now, he'd see the pink in her cheeks. All from a box of condoms. But, oh, the promise they held.

From the corner of her eye, Maggie saw a pair of tall blonde women in strapless tops and painted-on jeans checking out Hunter. Judging from their near-perfect bodies, the blondes did not have a linguine Alfredo problem.

Hunter released her elbow and pressed his palm flat against the bare skin on her back. He drew her closer until her hip brushed the side of his body. Instead of moving away from him, she leaned into his touch, enjoying the way her skin tingled. Half an inch lower and he would have touched the fabric of her shirt, but no, he'd opted for the intimate she's-mine touch.

"Honey, you're a helluva lot prettier," he murmured.

She glanced up at him and followed his gaze to the blonde Barbie look-alikes. "Thanks."

He smiled down at her. "Find your keys?"

"Right. The keys." His hand stayed firm against her skin, guiding her through the gate as she turned her attention back to her bag. But she could barely focus. Not when he was touching her. She'd never been so aware of a man, never had her imagination fast-forward to where his fingers would go next. Higher or lower?

The sounds of the car show faded as they made their way through the parking lot. "They're in here somewhere. I can drive. I know where the Marriott is—"

His hand fell away and she instantly missed the feel of him as he allowed her to step in front of him. Five minutes and they would be at the hotel. Five minutes and he'd be touching her again. If only she could find the key...

Warm breath tickled her neck and Maggie lost her train of thought.

"I'm going to kiss you now," he said. Soft fingertips swept her hair out of the way and then...lips. Soft, full lips.

Oh, God. Oh, my. Oh, yes...

She melted. His arm snaked around her waist, drawing her back against a hard wall of muscle. Sensation rushed down her body, settling into a warm ache as her knees went weak. He'd hit the perfect spot. He'd found the one place on the back of her neck, halfway between her shoulder and her hairline, that drove her mad with desire. Twelve months with Derrick and he'd never kissed her there, never turned her body to liquid need.

She pressed into the hard, muscled planes of his body, arching her back until her bottom rubbed against his crotch. She felt the hard evidence that he was just as turned on as she was. And feeling that, she wanted to be wild. She wanted to lose herself in a sea of excitement and desire. Her body was so alive it felt foreign. Was this really happening? To her?

Hunter sucked gently at the nape of her neck, keeping his hand pressed against her waist. *Higher,* she thought, *move your hand higher.* If he didn't touch her breasts soon, her nipples would burn holes in her shirt. Forget the hotel, she wanted him here. *Now.* Against the car.

As softly as he'd pulled her to him, he let go. She steadied herself against the driver's side door as her need slowly fell from an I-want-to-get-naked-with-you-in-the-parking-lot eleven to a nine.

"How about I drive," he said, his voice like gravel.

"Good idea." She managed to reach into her bag, her fingers searching, her mind unfocused from his kiss...and bingo. She withdrew the car key.

Like a man on a mission, he took her hand and quickly led her around to the passenger side. He unlocked her door and held it open as she slipped her giddy, excited body into the seat. But in the quiet car, away from him, her driving need faded and doubts seeped in. Maggie closed her eyes and clasped her hands together on her lap. She'd been seconds away from begging him to take her in the parking lot after a single kiss. What would happen once they were in his hotel room? Alone?

She didn't say a word as he drove to the Marriott and turned into the parking lot. Alan Jackson's "Gone Country" filled the car. *Not country,* she thought. *Crazy. Out of control.* She'd picked up a strange man at a car show, planned to have sex with him and told him as much. An hour ago she didn't even know his name.

Her right hand reached for the door, her fingers gliding back and forth over the electric lock button. Crazy. Plain and simple. Her plan, which had sounded brilliant earlier, now seemed insane and maybe even a little dangerous. There was a reason sane people went on dates, shared meals and engaged in hours of getting-to-know-you small talk. It was so they didn't fall into bed with a sinfully handsome man without knowing anything more than his name and occupation, that he liked nachos and could change a tire.

Oh, and he was a Ranger.

Maggie stole a quick glance at him and realized she knew more than what he'd revealed during their brief time together. Hunter Cross appeared to be a first-class gentleman and clearly knew his manners. He'd stood and held her chair. He'd opened the door for her. And he knew where to kiss her.

The memory of the kiss made the aching return. But was that enough? What if they got up to his room, she took off her clothes and he refused to wear a condom? She couldn't just walk out of his hotel room the next morning wondering if he'd gotten her pregnant or worse.

He put the car in Park near a side entrance. She kept her gaze fixed on the red exit sign above the hotel door, her hands shifting in her lap. She interlaced her trembling fingers and then released them.

"Maggie?"

"Hmm?"

"It's okay if you don't want to do this. I'll say goodnight and let you drive home. Or we can go inside to the hotel bar and have another water. Your call."

"No, I do." Interlaced fingers drummed against opposite hands. "I want this." *I want you. Badly.*

"Honey, your hands haven't stopped moving since we got in the car."

She released her grip and forced her fingers to lie still on her thighs.

"Nervous?" he asked gently.

"Yes." Fingernails digging into her jeans, she turned to him. "I think I left out a few important questions back at the fairgrounds."

He rested his arm on the center console and grinned. "I don't have a favorite color, but I love homemade lasagna."

"That's great, but I need to know more." The words tumbled forth as if she'd opened a floodgate, but she kept her eyes locked on her hands. "Like your medical history, and maybe a few references. And if you're allergic to latex."

He reached over and took her hand. His fingers wrapped around her palm and she felt the fear wane. She glanced up at him. If he was offended, she couldn't tell from his gentle smile.

"Maggie, I won't hurt you," he said seriously. "You have my word. I have condoms with me and I plan to use them if you're still interested. I swear on my father's grave that I have a clean bill of health. I just spent four weeks in a VA hospital followed by two months of inpatient therapy. They ran every test in the book and I'm clean."

"Why?"

"Gunshot." It was his turn to look at the exit sign.

"Oh, God." This was quickly becoming more complicated. Of all the men in the car show refreshment tent, she had to pick an injured Ranger. Depending on the extent of his injuries, the man sitting in the driver's seat of her rental car might never return to active duty.

"Are you sure you're up for this?" she asked.

Hunter laughed and smiled at her with his oh-so-handsome eyes. "Honey, I've been *up* for this since I first saw you at the bar."

"Oh." She glanced down at his thighs and saw the telltale bulge. The heat she'd felt when he kissed her neck returned full force. *I want that,* she thought. *Inside me, thrusting me over the cliff into orgasm territory.* Her excitement returned, but this time it was laced with something else. Power. She was the reason his pants were tight, probably uncomfortably so. And that inkling of control eased some of her fears.

"But if you've changed your mind, I will say good-night and go up to my room." He paused and she kept her gaze fixed on his lap. "I would much rather give you those orgasms you need."

"I don't want to leave." She withdrew her hand from his. "I just…I don't know where to start."

"Maggie. Look at me." She lifted her gaze. Their eyes met and Maggie forgot to breathe. She stared deeply into his brown eyes and she knew, just knew, she could trust this man—at least for tonight.

"Close your eyes," he said.

She obeyed.

"Now, tell me what you want, what you desire. Anything."

I want you to take charge. Tell me what to do. But she couldn't say that. No one had ever asked her what she wanted before. How could she reveal her fantasies to a virtual stranger? "I…I don't know."

"I think you do." He reclaimed her hand and traced soft circles with his thumb. She leaned closer. "What have you always wanted to do but never had the chance? I promise I won't laugh and you won't shock me."

"I don't know…." *How to put my fantasies into words.*

She heard a soft rustling and sensed him moving closer and then—lips. The soft, full lips that had tantalized her neck in the parking lot gently brushed the edge of her mouth. Capturing her lips with his, he kissed her slowly, as if he'd be content to stay here in her car all night. Just kissing.

But making out in the front seat didn't come close to fulfilling her fantasies. That was something the supposedly passionless Maggie would do—the Maggie who'd never shared her desires with the man she planned to marry. And right now? Passion threatened to short-circuit her brain. She leaned into him, hoping he'd take the hint and give her more.

Hunter did not disappoint. As far as first kisses went, this one was more of a conversation. He licked her lips as if asking, *Do you trust me?* Maggie opened her mouth slightly. His tongue swept inside, deepening the kiss, demanding to know if she was ready for more. As if he could sense her yielding, he stole his mouth away from hers.

"Tell me what you want," he said, his voice low and husky. "Or maybe there's something you don't want."

"I don't want to be in control." The words slipped out. "I just want to be and feel. Just for a little while."

He leaned in again and his lips touched her ear. "Lucky for you, I like to be the one calling the shots."

His tongue licked her earlobe and she groaned. Had she really said those words out loud? Really asked a man, a virtual stranger who could make a woman's panties wet with just one look, to take control in bed? What if he misunderstood? She didn't want to have to think or ask for what she needed; she just wanted him to know. But was that even possible? And what if he took charge by tying her to the bed? She might have a panic attack if she couldn't get up and leave.

But wasn't it time she finally let herself go? Maybe a little panic was good. Her carefully organized life would still be waiting for her in the morning.

"Come upstairs with me." It was a command, a gentle one, but she knew from his tone he'd taken over.

4

MAGGIE WATCHED HUNTER slip out of the car and walk around to open her door, offering his hand as he helped her out.

It was now or never. She could still turn back. But her body, her desire took over, and she placed her hand in his. Her gut told her this man could deliver. She was safe with him.

Following him through the side door and down the red-and-gold carpet to the elevator bank, Maggie pushed aside her doubts and fears. He was in control now—of her, her orgasms, everything. She could just let go.

He held the elevator door. "After you."

She stepped inside. There was no turning back now. She bit her lip as desire pooled in her belly and rushed lower.

"Maggie." He stepped toward her, pressing her against the mirrored back wall. "I'm going to kiss you now, and you're going to let me."

The door closed and his lips caught hers, a gentle brush, then hot and hard, his mouth devouring hers. This time he wasn't asking permission, he was taking and blazing the trail for his body to follow. She felt his hips press against her, his hands wrapping around her waist, holding her in place. His mouth left her wanting and wet, and his insistent body had her flexing her hips, returning the pressure. If she had any lingering uncertainty, it fell away, discarded on the elevator floor. And if they didn't get to his room soon, she feared her clothes would follow.

He pulled away slightly. "More, Maggie?"

She groaned and, leaning back against the mirrored wall, offered him access to her body. *Touch me there,* she thought. But she couldn't say the words, not yet, not here. In the elevator.

"Someone might see us," she mumbled.

"They might. Is that part of your fantasy?"

"No," she managed, still mesmerized by his touch.

"Then we better get you to the bedroom." His hand moved from her waist to the back of her thigh, leaving a trail of sensation. "Up you go."

He guided her leg upward until it wrapped around his waist. Then he lowered his other hand to her butt and lifted her off the floor. His lips found hers and he ground into her, pressing his hard length between her thighs.

The bell dinged and the door opened. Breaking the kiss, he turned and carried her out of the elevator and into the hall. Maggie closed her eyes and tried not to think about the grandmothers who might be wandering the hotel in search of ice. Instead, she ran her lips over his neck, nibbling the same place that he'd kissed earlier when she'd been pressed up against the car. Still holding her with one hand, he made his way along the hall. When he stopped, she felt herself pitch forward.

"Don't drop me," she said, drawing back to look at his face as he regained his balance and slipped his hand into his back pocket. His fingers brushed her calf in the process and Maggie squeezed her legs tighter. This man—he made her want and feel things she had thought out of her grasp. But here he was delivering them.

"We're here." Hunter smiled and slipped the card into the electronic reader.

He carried her into the room, kicking the door shut behind them before setting her on the bed.

"Take off your shirt," he said, standing over her, his dreamy eyes watching her with a wicked glint. "I've been dying to see your breasts since you sat down at my table."

Maggie had always been a rule follower, but occasionally she'd allowed for some creative interpretation. This was one of those times. Reaching for the bottom of her shirt, she ever so slowly began to lift. Inch by inch, she felt the cotton drift up over her belly.

Standing at the edge of the bed, Hunter stared, his eyes fixed on her hands, his chest rising and falling faster with each inch of skin she revealed. She watched his hands form tight fists at his sides.

"Higher," he commanded, his tone raw and deep.

Loving how she affected him, she drew the fabric up and over her breasts, feeling the soft tickle as her shirt teased her erect nipples. Arching forward, she silently begged him to claim her. He didn't move. Maggie pulled the shirt over her head and tossed it aside. Her nipples hardened further and her breasts ached to the point where if he didn't touch her soon, she might need to take matters into her own hands—literally.

"In my fantasy, I wasn't the only one undressed," she said softly, not wanting to strip away his control, but needing to see what lay beneath his clothes.

"I'd hate to fall short," he said, never taking his eyes off her chest.

"Impossible," she murmured as he pulled his green polo over his head and tossed it to the floor.

Her jaw dropped as she drank in the sight. Biceps that begged to be squeezed, broad shoulders, perfectly defined pecs that tapered off to a narrow waist—she'd wanted muscles and, heaven help her, he delivered, with a body that would put most male underwear models to shame. Maggie dug her fingers into the bedding to keep her hands from reaching out and touching his six-pack abs.

Her gaze followed the dark hair from below his navel to where it disappeared beneath where the waistband of his jeans hugged his hips. More. She wanted to see more of him. But she couldn't ask. She'd placed him in charge.

Forcing herself to look up, she saw the scarred flesh around his recent gunshot wound. It wasn't the only marking on his otherwise perfect body. Unlike most underwear models, his torso featured a jagged four-, maybe five-inch scar on his right side. But that one looked old compared to his shoulder wound. Both were vivid reminders of who this man was. A battle-worn soldier. Who knew what type of damage he had on the inside?

But not even that sobering thought could dim the hum of desire pulsing through her.

"My turn," he said, his low, lusty tone drawing her attention away from his recent injuries. "Your jeans, Maggie. Now."

This time, Maggie didn't waste any time. She slipped out of her heels and stripped off her jeans, pulling her underwear with them. Her hands moved swiftly, with confidence, and she reveled in the way her whole body hummed with anticipation. She sat at the edge of the bed, her feet resting on the soft carpet and her back stick-straight. Naked and waiting. She counted to ten. If he didn't move by the time she reached the magic number, she was reclaiming control, to hell with her fantasies.

Seven, eight, nine—

Hunter closed the gap and knelt by the foot of the bed, pushing her legs wide. Exposing her to his view. Maggie leaned back on her elbows. She saw the tension in his strong arms, his hands resting on her thighs, preventing her from closing her knees. She expected to feel embarrassed as he studied the most intimate parts of her body, but instead she became more turned on by the second.

"Beautiful," he murmured, his gaze moving up to settle on her breasts.

The slowness, the waiting, the needing was more than she could take. She'd never been this close to exploding without a man buried inside her. Maggie whimpered.

The corners of Hunter's lips hitched up as he leaned forward and caught her breast in his mouth. He took his time, sucking and running his tongue over her nipple, while his hand massaged her other breast. Pleasure pulsed through her entire body.

"I could stay here all night," he murmured. "With my face buried in your breasts."

"No," she groaned. "Please, I need more."

He looked up at her, his eyes promising she'd get what she wanted. "I thought I was in charge," he teased.

"You are," she gasped as his thumbs traced small circles on her nipples. "Just please don't stop."

Pressing her breasts together with his hands, he lowered his mouth and licked her cleavage before kissing his way back to her right nipple. Maggie cried out and rocked closer to him, eager to slide off the edge of the bed if that's what it took to get him inside of her.

"Easy, girl." She felt his words against her stomach as his mouth moved lower.

Keep going.

"Lie back and you'll get your orgasm." His breath tickled the curls between her legs and she obeyed, allowing his hands to push her up the mattress until her core was in the perfect position.

But he didn't kiss her there. Not yet. He took his time, running his hands up the insides of her thighs until his fingers grazed her outer folds. Maggie was aching now, pushing her body into his touch.

"Let me look," he demanded.

"Please," she begged, unable to find more words to ask for what she needed.

He found her most sensitive skin and she gasped, desperate now. Gently, tenderly, he teased her, running his thumb in small circles over her.

"You're so ready," he breathed. "And I thought I'd have to work to deliver your orgasms."

The hot, low sound of his voice nearly undid her.

"Not yet," he said, withdrawing his hand.

Maggie groaned. She'd been so close. To stop now—it was torture.

"Tell me where you like to be kissed." His lips brushed her inner thigh. "Here?"

"Yes," she whispered. "No. Higher."

"Here?" His tongue licked a path up her leg, stopping just short of where she needed him.

Maggie shifted her hips restlessly, but he held her firm.

"How about here?" His mouth skimmed her outer lips.

"Close, so close," she moaned.

He released her hip and used his hand to spread her wide. "Here?"

"Yes!" she screamed. His tongue licked her entrance, then up to the sensitive spot his fingers had toyed with moments earlier.

Closing her eyes, she lost herself to the feel of him exploring her, slowly at first, as if he wished to learn her body. She couldn't remember the last time anyone had made the effort to find what worked for her. Derrick never had. And then she forgot all other men. There was only Hunter, his mouth and his devilish hands. She cried out, trying for the word "yes" but only managing a high-pitched sound.

"Do you like that?" His finger pressed against her, but stopped before slipping inside. She moaned, arching up into his mouth. "Answer me."

"Yes," she gasped.

His tongue swirled back and forth over her wet folds, pushing her further toward the edge. She was so close. But what if it didn't happen? What if he'd gotten her this far, but couldn't get her over the edge? His mouth closed over her most sensitive flesh and she felt his finger slip inside her as he sucked mercilessly.

And then, she fell.

The orgasm that had been building since she'd first seen him at the bar swept over her. Bucking her hips against his mouth, she waited for him to pull back, for the pleasure to end. But he only moved his tongue faster, sliding it down to meet his fingers before gliding back up. She went higher, her whole body tingling with take-me-to-heaven bliss.

And when she finally came back down, he was still there with her, his hands touching her, his mouth worshipping her. Maggie pushed herself up onto her elbows and looked down at him. She tried to think of something to say, but "you can stop now" seemed just plain wrong and "amazing" just wasn't enough. Instead, she reached down and touched his soft brown hair.

Hunter lifted his head, smiling, his eyes filled with heat. He rocked back and sat on his heels, watching her.

She drew her knees together, allowing her legs to fall to one side, the pressure of her inner thighs against each other sending delicious aftershocks through her body.

"One down," he said, rising from his crouched position at the foot of the bed. "Are you ready for another?"

"THERE'S MORE," SHE WHISPERED. It wasn't a question. Simply a statement issued with wide-eyed wonder.

"We're just getting started."

Hunter watched her blue eyes scan his bare chest. Had a woman ever looked at him with such earnest amazement? He reached for the button on his jeans and Maggie followed the movement, her lips parted. Wanting to draw this out, he paused, admiring the view in front of him— blond hair tousled, breasts that he knew for a fact overflowed his hands, shapely legs turned to one side, offering a view of her round backside. He wanted her, every inch, but the sexy yet innocent look on her face? That drove him wild. He needed to be inside her.

Without taking his eyes off her, he knelt down and quickly removed his boots. He stripped off his jeans and reached for the elastic band on his boxer briefs. All the while Maggie watched him. He paused. Condom. He needed protection. Now. Once he took off his shorts, there was no turning back.

He withdrew a foil packet from his wallet and stripped off his last piece of clothing. A soft gasp drew his attention back to the bed. Maggie stared at his hard-on. There was appreciation in that look and something else he couldn't quite put his finger on.

"If you're worried it won't fit, I can assure you it will, but you can go ahead and say the words anyway," Hunter teased.

"You're huge," Miss Maggie whispered.

"You certainly know your lines." He tore open the foil packet and covered himself, then lay down beside her on the bed.

"Compared to my last—"

"Let's not bring him in here right now. Just you and me."

Running his hand up her thigh to her hip, he gave her a gentle push and rolled her onto her back. He kissed her, supporting his weight on his arms as he hovered over her body. "I can't wait much longer," he said against her lips. "I want you. Fast and hard."

"Yes," she gasped, arching up until her nipples brushed his chest.

Hunter leaned back and positioned himself at her entrance. He couldn't wait. Next time, he'd make love to her slowly, but not now. The need was driving him wild. He couldn't remember the last time he'd been this close to losing control with a woman. And one he'd just met? Never.

Her fingers touched his covered cock, wrapping around him as if she wished to help him find his way.

"May I?" she asked.

He nodded. Her soft voice made him throb as she guided him into her very tight heat. How long had it been for her? The thought floated through his mind and drifted away. God help him, Little Miss Maggie felt impossibly good. He began the familiar pull and push as her hips rose up to meet him thrust for thrust.

But missionary just wasn't doing it for him. He wanted more.

"Turn over."

Maggie opened her eyes and he watched as she processed his command. Reaching for a couple of pillows, he positioned them under her hips as she rolled. Kneeling behind her raised backside, he slipped inside and thrust. Deeply. And then he let go. Listening to her moans, her begging sounds demanding more, he knew she was on board and ready to come with him. He pounded against her, losing himself to the chaotic movements.

Beneath him, Maggie arched, taking him deeper still. And then she screamed, smacking the sheets with one hand as she begged for more. He'd never felt a woman come apart with such abandon. It nearly undid him. But he couldn't let that happen. Not yet.

He leaned forward, releasing her bucking hips as he reached around to touch the spot he knew would skyrocket her to the peak of her second orgasm. And this time, he came with her.

MAGGIE ROLLED OFF the stack of pillows, taking one with her. Cuddling it against her chest, she closed her eyes and reveled in the orgasmic shock waves still pulsing through her body. She'd never had sex like that—wild, unrestrained—the way she wanted it. If she'd been home in her own bed, she might have thought she was dreaming. But she wasn't in her empty mansion. The pillow against her chest belonged to the Marriott hotel. Nothing in this room, apart from her clothes, belonged to her, including Hunter. None of it was her responsibility.

She waited for the disappointment, but it didn't come. Instead, relief snuggled up next to her. After tonight, after another round or two, she'd never see him again. She had a Toyota parked outside and she planned to use it.

Maggie sighed into her borrowed bedding.

"Give me that." Hunter plucked the pillow from her grasp and tossed it off the bed. "You're making me jealous of a pile of goose feathers."

"I'm pretty sure these are synthetic." Maggie wrapped her body around his, letting her head lie on his shoulder. He tensed beneath her. Opening her eyes, she saw him wince. The gunshot wound. She'd completely forgotten. She sat up. "Am I hurting you?"

"My shoulder aches sometimes, usually after a workout." He sat up beside her on the bed. "And that was quite a workout."

A warm flush crept up her cheeks. He'd given her everything she'd needed. It only seemed fair that she offer him something in return. "Would you like a massage? I'm not a professional. Not even close. But I'll give it my best shot."

"Oh, yeah, I'm definitely going to take you up on that. But first let's order some grub." Smiling, he flopped down on his back and reached for the hotel phone on the nightstand. "Turns out those nachos weren't enough. I need to refuel. Up for a late-night snack?"

Maggie glanced at the clock. It was only ten. But if he was hungry, she could pick at something while he ate. "Sure."

"Great." He rolled to his side and pressed the button for room service. Maggie listened as he ordered two pasta dishes, a salad and a dessert. Then he asked the person on the other end to hold.

"Are you a vegetarian?" he asked her, his hand over the receiver.

"No, and no dessert for me." If he was going to look at her thighs again after their "snack," she didn't want to wonder if hotel cheesecake had added an extra layer.

Suddenly self-conscious, Maggie went to the bathroom and found two plush robes while Hunter finished ordering. She wrapped one around her still tingling body and returned to the room to offer him the other. He took it without pointing out that he'd already seen her naked, or saying he preferred to remain unclothed. *A perfect gentleman,* she thought, except when he'd taken her from behind. Then he'd been pure animal.

She smiled. He would make some woman very happy

one day, but not her. This man was too I'm-in-charge for her world. Maggie sat back down on the bed.

"So tell me, Maggie," he said. She tensed, waiting for him to ask her about her work, or her home, or why she'd been on the prowl for a one-night stand. "What is your favorite Italian restaurant?"

Maggie laughed her relief. "The Olive Garden."

He nodded, accepting her choice instead of demanding to know why a woman who could afford to eat at Mario Batali's finest New York City establishments any night of the week would pick a chain.

"Mine's this small hole-in-the-wall in Costa Rica," he said. "I was down there on vacation a few years back, on the Caribbean side, when I found it. Had to walk down an unlit road to get there, but it was worth it."

The food arrived and the conversation flowed. They talked about travel and vacations, but never work or home life. She told him how she'd fallen in love with Italy when she was seventeen and visiting on a school trip. He told her about his favorite Greek island, Antiparos. They talked until she'd devoured half the salad (he ignored the other half), a third of a meat-filled lasagna (he ate the rest) and a bit of the vegetarian penne.

He barely touched the wine he'd ordered, sticking mostly to water, she noted, before pushing the thought from her mind. Now was not the time or place to study his behavior or compare him to her father. Tonight was for pleasure, and so far, the evening had exceeded her expectations. Sipping her own glass of white wine, Maggie thought, *This is the best date of my life. And it's not even a real date.*

BESIDE HIM ON the bed, Maggie leaned back against a mountain of pillows. Forget Greece, he had his very own goddess right here. Her loose curls rested on the plush robe. *Take it off,* he thought. *I want to touch you again.*

He drained the last of his water and set the glass on the room service table while Maggie described her dream vacation: Paris. He'd only met her a few hours earlier, and in reality he knew very little about her, but he still felt closer to her than he had to most of the women he'd dated in the past few years. And he wondered if it was because she didn't try so hard. She wasn't here to find forever or to prove they were a good fit. She was just here because she wanted sex. If the erection under his robe was any indication, it was about time for another round. But first, she'd promised him a massage.

Hunter rolled his shoulder. Sex mingled with half a glass of wine had dulled the ache, but it was still there. "About that massage, you still game?"

"Oh, yes." She sat up, transforming instantly from relaxed beauty to take-charge woman. Little Miss Maggie reminded him of a Rubik's Cube, her colors constantly changing. One minute her yellow, innocent side shone bright, then a row moved, adding a touch of brazen red. And when she came, hands slapping the bedding? That's when all the colors mixed together.

Hunter shrugged out of his robe and flopped down on his stomach, turning his head to the side to watch Maggie. She set her wine on the night table and crawled across the bed. "I don't think you can give a proper massage with your robe on."

"Is that an order?" She raised an eyebrow.

"Yes, ma'am." The side of his mouth hitched upward. "If that's what it takes to get you naked."

Maggie laughed as she loosened the fabric belt at her waist and unwrapped her lush curves. He didn't want to take his eyes off her full, perky breasts, enjoying the slight rise and fall with each breath she took. But when she shifted to straddle his lower back, he wasn't left with a choice. Her hands touched his aching shoulder, gently, yet exerting just enough pressure to push away the pain. The rest of the world slipped out of reach, leaving behind Maggie's hands, her heat grazing his lower back. When he died, if Hunter could have his pick of heavens, he'd return to this moment.

Ten, maybe fifteen minutes into the massage, the brazen Miss Maggie replaced her hands with her lips. Kissing and licking, she made her way down the center of his back, shimmying her wet core over his ass as she moved lower and lower....

He moaned.

"Roll over," she whispered against his skin. "Please."

Not caring who was in charge anymore, he obeyed, wondering if he would come the moment she touched him. Definite possibility. He opened his eyes and watched as she knelt beside him. Meeting his gaze as if she wanted permission, she asked, "May I?"

"Hell, yes."

Her tongue licked the length of his shaft and his hips lifted up, demanding more. She gave it to him, wrapping her mouth around him. Her tongue swirled up and down, and Hunter dug his hands into the sheets. He swallowed a whimper when her lips rose to the tip. Then she wrapped her hand around one of his and lowered her mouth again. He closed his eyes and prayed the sensation would never end.

Minutes later, he knew he was too close to finding his release, and he didn't want to come like this. Not without her. Gently, he pushed her away. "Lie down."

Maggie stretched out on the bed beside him. "I wasn't finished."

"Some other time. Right now, there's something else I want from you. You put me in charge. I'm calling the shots." He retrieved a condom from the box he'd placed on the nightstand before dinner and quickly covered himself.

"Something new?"

Staring into her eyes, he hovered above her. "Honey, I could teach you things that would blow your fantasies out of the water. But right now, I just need you."

His lips touched hers and he pushed inside. And this time, he filled her slowly, making love to her with everything he had left to give.

When she shattered beneath him, a little voice in the back of his consciousness whispered, *Please don't let this be the last time*. And then he came, forgetting everything but Maggie and this moment.

HOURS LATER, HUNTER opened one eye, not sure he could move another muscle. He watched Maggie quickly slip into her clothes, then reach into her bag and pull out a pair of flip-flops. *So much more her style than those shiny white things,* he thought. But then it hit him. Shoes meant she was leaving, making a run for it while he slept.

He waited for her to dig a pen and paper out of her bag. After the night they'd shared, he knew she wouldn't disappear without a goodbye or, more likely, a let's-get-together-soon note. But instead, she picked up the white heels and tried to fit them into her purse. When the shiny shoes refused to disappear into the depths of her bag on the first try, she gave them one last look—a goodbye glance—and abandoned them on the floor beside the desk.

He didn't move. She'd spared a parting moment for her shoes, but not him. She was leaving, sneaking out before dawn, and he couldn't stop her. Hell, even if he let her know he was awake, he wouldn't have a clue what to say. He usually did the sneaking, not the other way around.

He watched her tiptoe to the door, careful not to let her flip-flops smack her heels for the first few steps, but then panic seemingly took over and she ran for the exit like a spooked horse. He waited for a backward glance. For the first time in as long as he could remember, he wanted more—a phone number scrawled on an old receipt or written in lipstick across his chest.

He wanted a promise of one more night before he left town. Something. Anything.

But Little Miss Maggie didn't look back as she slipped out of the room.

5

Sipping his overpriced hotel coffee, Hunter stood by the Marriott side entrance waiting for his commanding officer to pick him up. Lieutenant Colonel Walt Johnson had flown in yesterday for this morning's mystery meeting, but had opted to stay with an old friend from West Point.

And wasn't that a damn shame. Not that he was particularly close to his commanding officer. Colonel Johnson was too caught up in army politics in Hunter's opinion. But his CO gave the orders and Hunter followed them. Occasionally, they got together for a beer. Too bad the colonel wasn't available last night. Hunter could have used the distraction.

Everywhere he looked in this damn hotel, from the elevator to the inside of his room, he thought of Maggie, the woman he'd never see again. He'd spent most of Sunday in the Marriott's indoor pool, trying to exhaust his body, so it wouldn't ache for her. He loved to swim. He'd almost joined the navy, but had decided he owed it to his old man to follow in his footsteps and go army.

But yesterday it had been pure punishment. After a dozen laps in, his shoulder had throbbed, desperate for another one of Maggie's not-quite-professional massages.

And he didn't just want the massage; he wanted the happy ending to go with it. One night of bed-shaking, mind-blowing sex had left him walking around with a hard-on that just wouldn't quit and a pair of white heels he couldn't bring himself to throw out. Go figure.

A red Mustang convertible pulled into the hotel parking lot. Johnson. The man liked his cars. Who wouldn't want the wind in their hair on a sunny summer day?

Hunter took one last sip of his coffee before ditching the cup in the trash. It was time to work. Time to put Saturday night behind him.

"Colonel." Hunter opened the passenger-side door and took a seat.

"Chief. How's the shoulder?"

"Just fine, sir." *Ready for active duty. Please, God, send me back now.*

"This mission should provide you with plenty of time for R & R. And you're going to need it. Nail this one and that promotion, head of the Alpha Team? It's yours." His CO dropped a manila folder on his lap and put the car in gear. "The official briefing materials."

"Thank you, sir." Hunter smiled for the first time since Saturday night. Leader of the Alpha Team. A promotion. His dream job and a bigger paycheck. Whatever it was the colonel needed done, he'd do it. Hunter broke the envelope's seal.

"Nothing but official crap in there." His CO steered the Mustang out of the parking lot. "Just says your job here is to play nice with a political science professor named Margaret Barlow. Do a few interviews this week, set up a few more with your teammates."

A week with a professor? His smile faded.

"Ms. Barlow is writing a book about your latest mission. Top brass believes she wants to focus too much attention on what went wrong during the rescue you boys pulled off while riding those damn horses."

"And they gave her the go-ahead to look into it?" Hunter had been laid up in the hospital at the time, but he knew there had been questions about his last mission. Specifically, how he'd ended up with a bullet in his shoulder. The extraction had been a disaster. His teammate had been too distracted to cover him, his mind still on the wife he'd buried before they'd deployed, and Hunter had taken a bullet. Better him than the aid worker he'd been carrying to safety at the time.

"Top brass granted her access because her old man was a decorated Ranger. He came home injured and received a medal or two for his actions. The generals don't want the press to find out we denied a decorated war vet's daughter access."

"Can't afford to say no." Hunter nodded. "I get it."

"But we also can't let this woman run hog wild, writing whatever she damn pleases about what you boys did over there." The colonel sped through a yellow light. "After the SEAL debacle, with that one soldier publishing a goddamn outline of the bin Laden mission, a memo came down from the top about letting classified information—hell, any substantive information about how we work—get out into the public. And the last thing we need is a public record of our mistakes."

Hunter nodded, his jaw clenched. This mission reeked of internal politics and if he had a choice he'd say *count me out, sir.* He'd rather jump out of a helo than read some goddamn manuscript any day. But he knew the colonel well enough to know this assignment wasn't optional.

"You won't find it written up in the paperwork," his CO continued. "But your job is to control what goes in her book. Act as her liaison, set up interviews with your teammates, but be damn sure you've coached the boys on what to say. Let her ask you a few questions and lead her away from sensitive issues. With the details of the SEAL's mission out there in print, we can't afford to be the next Special Forces group to spill our guts to the public. Stonewall her. Distract her. I don't care. Just keep the upper hand and be certain you've read her drafts before she sends them off to her fancy New York publisher. Succeed and you're the new team leader. I'll have you shipping out with your team as soon as this is over."

"Yes, sir." Give a few interviews, distract a professor from telling the public about his teammate's mistake and receive the job he'd always wanted and the money to take care of his sister? It sounded like a win-win. Everything he'd ever wanted was being handed to him on a platter.

Except Maggie.

When was the last time a one-night stand had distracted him from doing his job and protecting his family? Try never. He didn't look back. Never wanted more. Sierra and the thrill of his job were enough for him. But somehow Miss Maggie had gotten under his skin. Or maybe it was the boredom from being sidelined from missions that were more exciting than babysitting and reading books. If he couldn't deploy with his team, fulfilling Maggie's fantasies was the next best thing.

On the bright side, a week, maybe more, in upstate New York 100 percent increased his chances of running into Miss Maggie again. She lived around here somewhere and he did have her shoes.

But he'd have some old professor with him. Might not help his chances for getting laid again.

"She's practically a child," his CO said, turning into the West Point main entrance. Hunter tuned his attention back to his mission. "It shouldn't take much to keep her under control."

"Yes, sir." Okay, so the professor didn't sound ancient. But with Colonel Johnson, one never knew. Any woman under forty was practically a child in his mind.

His CO spun the wheel, guiding them into a parking spot, and turned to him. "I'm counting on you for this one."

"I'm on it, sir." Hunter opened his door and followed his CO into one of West Point's castle-like buildings, ready to meet Margaret Barlow, complete his mission and earn his promotion and pay raise.

MAGGIE ADJUSTED HER boxy gray suit jacket, checked her PowerPoint presentation and scanned the conference-room table to make sure the packets she'd prepared were in front of each seat. As she straightened her presentation notes on the podium, her mind drifted to Saturday night. It had been perfect, really. A handsome stranger, orgasms—three of them—and the freedom to return to her world on Sunday morning.

Perfect.

Well, almost.

The side of her mouth drooped. Hunter had satisfied something deep inside her, but he'd also left her feeling helpless. An hour after he'd fallen asleep, panic had washed over her. She'd escaped as fast as she could, even though part of her—the part that craved orgasms—wanted to know just what he'd meant when he'd said the words that played through her mind on repeat.

Honey, I could teach you things that would blow your fantasies out of the water.

She wanted to learn those things, and she wanted to learn them from him, which scared her even more than the way she'd followed his commands in bed. Hunter was the worst possible match for her. She needed stable and dependable, not commanding.

Plus, she didn't have the first clue what sort of demons Hunter had faced in his personal life since his return from the war. The writer in her might be curious, but the part of her that wanted to savor the memory of those orgasms? That part of her needed to remember him just the way he was Saturday night. Let someone else deal with his depression and the potential drinking and drug problems when he tried to adapt to a normal life. Let him send someone else's life spiraling out of control. She'd been there and done that. She had no intention of going back. Not even for the best orgasms in the world.

Of course, setting aside the fact that he was an elite soldier, once they got to know each other, it probably wouldn't work. Maggie glanced down at her plain black flats, nearly hidden by her gray slacks. Scratch probably and make that definitely. If he saw her now, he wouldn't even recognize her, never mind date her. He certainly wouldn't demand she remove her clothes. Not this shapeless suit, which was exactly why'd she'd worn it to her meeting and not out for her wild Saturday night.

In this room, surrounded by a group of men who could put an end to her book before she even got a chance to write it, she couldn't afford to look like a sexy, single woman. She needed them to listen to her, not stare at her breasts like a pack of hormonal boys. Today, in this suit, she could not be caught thinking about the best orgasms of her life. These men would know the minute they set foot in the room if she was thinking about sex. And then they'd never take her seriously. Not that they were doing so now.

Their chosen space showed the top brass's interest in her book. Instead of a conference room inside West Point proper, they'd placed her in a trailer-turned-meeting-room.

Sure, it held a podium, a screen for her PowerPoint and a conference table, but it was still a singlewide that could be disposed of any minute.

The trailer door opened with a whine and a middle-aged gray-haired man in dress uniform stepped in. "Are you ready for us, Ms. Barlow?"

Maggie plastered a serious expression on her face and gripped the sides of the podium. "Yes, please come in."

Three men, all over fifty if they were even that young, filed into the room and took their seats. Not one of them offered an introduction or a handshake. They assumed she knew who they were, which she did, and that was fine with her. She preferred thinking of them as the pointy-nosed general, the stone-faced one and the pudgy one.

The stone-faced man, who sat closest to the podium, looked up at her. "We're expecting two more."

As if on cue, the door creaked open.

"Ms. Barlow, this is Lieutenant Colonel Walt Johnson from Fort Campbell in Tennessee, and Chief Warrant Officer Hunter Cross from the army ranger's Seventy-Fifth Division. Provided we like what we hear today, Chief Cross will act as your liaison while you conduct your interviews."

The trailer door closed behind the man who'd knelt between her spread legs and given her the most powerful orgasm of her life. Hunter. Maggie's face burned and her knees turned to noodles.

"Ms. Barlow," Hunter said, his eyes wide with surprise and something else she couldn't quite read.

Dear God, that voice sent shock waves through her body down to her core, and a place deep inside her that had no business attending a meeting in her conservative suit melted. Then she came crashing back to reality.

Hunter, her one-night stand, was her army liaison? This

man, who'd spent Saturday night fulfilling her sexual fantasies, held the key to her success?

Oh, hell. Oh, holy crap.

Maggie closed her eyes and took a deep breath in through her nose and out through her mouth. He wouldn't say a word. Not Hunter, the man who held doors and pulled out chairs. The man she'd met at the car show would never open his mouth and say, "Hey, Maggie, thanks for Saturday night. I hope you got all the orgasms you needed." No, he would not do that.

She hoped. She prayed.

But he didn't need to say anything to throw her off her presentation. Just the sight of him made her think of sex. Okay, so she wouldn't look at him. She'd pretend he wasn't there. She could do this. She had to do this. If she ran out of the trailer now, she'd never get another meeting with these men.

Opening her eyes, Maggie plastered a serious smile on her face, not too big or too charming, but just enough so that she did not appear combative. Gripping the sides of the podium, she waited for Chief Hunter Cross and Lieutenant Colonel what's-his-name to take their seats. Then she looked down at the podium and began the most important presentation of her career.

HUNTER STEPPED INTO the dinky trailer and froze as if approaching a land mine. *Maggie.* He didn't need C4 to knock him on his ass; shock nearly did the trick. His orgasm-demanding one-night stand stood at the podium.

He reached for the back of his chair, pulled it out from the table and sat before he fell. Maybe it wasn't the same woman. Maybe his Maggie had a poorly dressed, too-serious twin.

Her fingers drummed the side of the podium and a faint

blush spread across her face. Nope. Same Maggie. And she'd recognized him, too. Judging from the color on her cheeks, she was probably thinking the same thing he was: less than forty-eight hours ago, they'd been naked together. In bed. Exploring her fantasies.

Hunter smiled and wondered what he'd done to deserve this divine twist of fate. He'd been assigned to spend the next week, maybe longer, with the woman who'd rocked his world with her demand for orgasms. Plural. It didn't matter that his vibrant, multicolored Rubik's Cube had turned gray on all sides. He knew what lay under that god-awful, ugly suit—a woman who pummeled the bed as she came. With that crystal clear memory, surprise morphed into an I'm-so-getting-laid-again feeling.

"What did I tell you?" his commanding officer muttered, leaning over from the seat beside his. "She's just a girl."

Like hell she is, Hunter thought.

"It won't take much to keep her on a tight leash." The colonel slapped him on the shoulder and turned to the man on his other side.

Control her. That was his objective. The getting-laid happy feeling turned up a notch. Wasn't that what Maggie had begged for Saturday night? For him to take control? Sure, she'd been talking about sex, but of all the women he'd ever met, Miss Maggie was the most likely to follow his orders both in bed and when it came to her book.

Images from Saturday night flashed in his mind like a highlight reel. Hunter's smile fell as he reached the end, where she walked, no, make that ran, for the door. If she'd been so into it, why had she run away while she thought he was sleeping?

He glanced up at the woman behind the podium, the only woman in the room. It took balls to stand up in front of decorated generals. A woman like that didn't hand over control of her work. And if he tried to take it? No way she'd invite him back into her bed.

"Good morning, gentlemen." Maggie's steady voice cut through the room, silencing the muttering generals. Hunter watched her face, but she didn't look up. Not once. She kept her gaze glued to her notes. She sounded confident, but he knew better. Her hands moved a mile a minute against the side of the podium. Bold and nervous, that was his Maggie. Except he had a sinking feeling she wasn't his now and she wouldn't be anytime soon.

"Thank you for your time." The first slide appeared on the screen behind her. "'America's Cowboy Heroes,'" she read. "My book focuses on the team that completed a successful mission without the aid of most modern warfare tools, including cars. The men who rescued three aid workers while riding horses provided by an Afghan warlord."

Cowboys? Hunter rolled his sore shoulder. He might have ridden a horse through the Afghan mountains, but he'd done it out of necessity. If he'd been driving a tank when he was sent in to save those women, he wouldn't have gotten shot, with or without his teammate's error. But their friendly Afghan warlord host hadn't exactly shown up at the meeting point with a fleet of armored vehicles.

"There is no argument that the modern-day cowboys who went out of their way to save those women are heroes," she continued.

Maggie clicked a button and a photo Hunter remembered all too well from a national newspaper appeared on the screen—a picture of his team covered in dust, riding those damn horses. His jaw tightened. He didn't like where she was going with this. If their faces hadn't been covered with bandannas, with only their eyes showing, that picture could have seriously affected his ability to do his job. The last thing he needed was a target on his back when he entered hostile territory.

"America wants to hear their story," she said. "Similar to the accounts of the navy SEAL mission that eliminated enemy number one, I plan to take a detailed look at the Rangers' ride and take the readers through these heroes' actions step-by-step."

Johnson shifted in his seat and sent Hunter a pointed look. Hunter met his commanding officer's gaze. *Message read, loud and clear, sir. Walk her through it without revealing details. Glaze over Logan's mistake.*

Hunter frowned. It was a crappy assignment. While his teammates hunted the enemy, he had to give interviews to a writer who thought he'd endured years of grueling training to become a damn cowboy. And to make a shitty situation worse, that writer had to be the one woman who'd left him wanting more.

"Look, Ms. Barlow, we're prepared to give you access to the team of Rangers who completed this mission, provided Chief Cross acts as your liaison and you answer a few questions." Major General Patterson spoke from his seat beside the podium. Hunter knew of the man. Based out of Fort Bragg, Patterson commanded the Special Forces teams, and his hard-ass reputation was legendary.

At the podium, Maggie smiled, and this time it touched her eyes. She thought she'd won, Hunter realized. If only she knew that working with him wasn't going to be the all-access pass she had in mind.

"Do you honestly believe anyone will want to read your book?" Major General Patterson challenged.

"Yes, I do. I wouldn't waste your time otherwise. The American public is fascinated by this story. When that picture was published, it was one of the most viewed items of the week. Working with my publisher, I've already begun using social media outlets to build on that excitement. Soon I will also be launching a blog to keep my readers interested until the book is available."

A blog about his mission? Hunter's frown sank into a scowl. Yeah, that wouldn't go over well.

"I assure you, I intend to write a book that will sell," Maggie continued, her voice steady. "This book is important to me on a professional level, yes, but also on a personal level. Both my father and my grandfather fought for our country, and I plan to donate my royalties to charities that support veterans as they transition from war to everyday life."

Across the table, one of the generals raised an eyebrow, as if to say *who gives a rat's ass what you plan to do with your money?* Hunter turned his attention back to Maggie, watching her hands. This time they didn't move. She just held on tight to the podium. She should be shitting in her pants right now, her hands fluttering like a hummingbird on speed. But nope, not this time. Not one sign of nerves.

She was in her element here, he realized. This was the real Maggie. Not the soft, give-me-orders woman he'd met Saturday night. The woman standing in front of him got under his skin, but not in a good way, not like his Little Miss Maggie from the car show. And the more she talked about how she wanted to turn his team into America's Cowboy Heroes, the less he liked her.

"My publisher is excited," Maggie said, looking directly at Patterson. "They agree with my strong belief that now is the perfect time to publish this book."

"Yes, but your publisher is in business to make money," General Patterson said. "We're not. The United States Army has a duty to keep their soldiers safe. Once you reveal the details of our missions, what will prevent the enemy from placing our soldiers at the top of their hit list?"

The general's words sank in. The idea that with a swish of her pen Maggie could prevent Hunter from doing the job he loved, from earning a living to support his sister, set his teeth on edge. He didn't care how great she was in bed.

"I understand your concerns," Maggie replied. "In my previous book, I used pseudonyms. The marines I interviewed felt this was fair and they were a pleasure to work with, as I'm sure your men will be."

He heard the challenge underlying her sugar-sweet words loud and clear. "Ms. Barlow," Hunter said. She looked at him for the first time since he'd sat down at the table. If he was going to take control, why not start now? Before she launched her blog. Before she skyrocketed him to the top of the Taliban's kill list.

"Yes?"

He heard a hint of uncertainty in her voice for the first time since he'd entered the trailer.

"Forget about the marines." He smiled, allowing his eyelids to fall slightly. Beside him, his colonel snickered, a sentiment echoed around the table. There wasn't a man in here who didn't know about Hunter's orders, or his reputation with women. "Working with me will blow those guys out of the water."

6

WORKING WITH ME will blow those guys out of the water.

Three generals, one colonel, her Saturday-night lover and the fate of her book stared at Maggie, waiting for her response. She blinked, allowing silence to fill the so-called meeting room. Her mind processed his words, but her body? It only heard a sigh-worthy promise that reminded her of Saturday night. From the tingling place on the back of her neck to the tips of her toes, she felt his words like the precursor to one of his oh-heaven-help-me orgasms.

Judging from his sensual tone, he remembered his promise, too. And now he was using it against her. He was trying to derail her presentation with barely concealed sexual references. From the smug look on his face, he was waiting to see if she'd melt into a puddle of take-me-over-the-conference-table need.

But she refused to let the generals see how Hunter's words affected her. The men at the table might not know about her prior relationship with her army-issued liaison, but decades of military service had fine-tuned their ears for suggestive comments. She'd spent years studying the military. She knew how these guys worked.

Maggie couldn't afford to screw up now. She had to se-

cure interviews with these Rangers or there wouldn't be
a book. Her publisher wouldn't be happy about that. And
without a book, she wouldn't make tenure. She could kiss
the promise of a secure future goodbye. Unless she maintained control of the meeting and her liaison.

The silence in the trailer stretched out, bordering on
uncomfortable. She had to say something, but *I'm never
going to sleep with you again* wouldn't help her cause.

"Thank you, Chief. Let's hope that is the case. With
my deadline only months away, we'll have to work fast."
Maggie met his I-want-to-see-you-naked gaze. What had
happened to her Saturday-night gentleman? Had that been
an act? Probably. "Your cooperation will make the interviews much smoother."

"I won't disappoint you," he said.

Beneath her work clothes, her body thrilled at the promise those words held. *Not going there,* Maggie reminded
herself as she turned her attention to the generals. It was
time to wrap up before the top brass began placing bets
on how long it would take Hunter to seduce her. They'd
all lose unless someone put money on *been there, done
that and left my shoes behind.*

"I know your time is valuable and you are anxious to
return to your duties." Maggie made a point to look at
each man sitting at the table except Hunter. "Thank you
for sharing your thoughts. I'm sure Chief Cross will keep
you updated on my progress. Have a good day, gentlemen."

She smiled as they stood and filed toward the door. The
pointy-nosed general muttered a word of thanks for her
"insightful" presentation. Another said he looked forward
to hearing more from her after she'd completed her interviews. Judging from his tone, he'd rather have a root canal.

Hunter's handler—his commanding officer—beamed
at her. "Great job, great job." *Yeah, right.*

"Winning the generals' approval is no small task," the colonel continued.

Maggie frowned. They had capitulated fairly quickly. Was she missing something? She pushed that thought away, focusing on the colonel and her liaison.

"Chief Cross is at your disposal. He will meet you by the front gate once you've gathered your things here."

"Thank you, sir," Maggie managed to reply. "A pleasure meeting you."

"Likewise." He smirked, letting the trailer door slam behind him.

She waited for Hunter to follow. It was just the two of them in the trailer now. Unless he wanted to discuss Saturday night, which Maggie wasn't ready for, not yet, her freshly issued liaison should be following his superiors out the door.

Instead, Hunter took a step forward and leaned in, his mouth moving toward the side of her head. For a split second, she thought he would kiss her neck and she froze.

He couldn't possibly want her. Not dressed like this. But that hot place deep inside didn't care about her clothes. *Kiss me,* her body demanded.

"I'll bring your shoes," he whispered, his breath tickling the precise spot on her neck that drove her crazy. Touch-me-now sensations rippled from her neck down to her breasts before settling between her legs.

Maggie closed her eyes and prayed he would leave. Part of her wanted to follow those sensations to their natural end, but the part of her that had kept her life moving forward when her father fell apart knew she couldn't. She could not sleep with him and at the same time interview him for her book. It would undermine her credibility. And if the tenure committee found out? She'd be out of a job. She refused to fail. Determination welled deep inside her and Maggie clung to it. No orgasms. Not from Chief Hunter Cross. Not while they were working together.

The door creaked. Footsteps followed, and then, thank heavens, the door closed.

Maggie opened her eyes. She was alone. Finally. She marched over to the podium to pack her laptop and notes. She'd survived the meeting. The generals didn't believe her book would be worth reading—judging from his comments, General Patterson wouldn't use it as a doorstop—but she'd made it to the end without running from the room. And more important, she'd secured their support. Mostly. The one man whose cooperation she truly needed had just offered a seductive look paired with a sigh-worthy promise.

Maggie closed the laptop with more force than necessary, but she couldn't help it. Her Nervous Nellie hands were tense with irritation. Was this a joke to him, his assignment as her liaison? Or did he seriously plan to use his position and proximity to get her into bed?

She needed his help. It wasn't as if she could demand another liaison. What would she say? *Sorry, fellas, I already slept with this one and then I left him before the sun came up. Without a note.*

Her arm froze midair and her index cards fluttered to the ground. Oh, God. What if he was pissed off about her walking away without a goodbye? What if he was trying to retaliate?

Maggie reached forward and held on to the podium, her mind racing. If she was right, this wasn't about desire. A man like Hunter did not go for women in baggy suits. But if she'd bruised his ego, she'd bet her career he would try to even the score. He wasn't stupid. He'd picked up on the generals' distaste for her work and probably thought *why not kill two birds with one stone?* Win the top brass's approval and take out the woman who'd walked out on him while he'd slept.

For all she knew, he might be giving his CO the play-by-play of Saturday night right now. Maggie felt her cheeks flush. She could wear the ugliest gray suit in her closet and these men would never take her seriously again, not if they knew she'd asked a virtual stranger at a car show for wild, passionate sex. Nope, she would never get another liaison. And her book? If she couldn't do the research, there wouldn't be a book.

She had to work with Hunter. She would find a way to manage him.

AT PRECISELY 1100 HOURS, Hunter approached the gate with a white plastic bag labeled Marriott in one hand and his duffel bag over his shoulder. Now that he was sticking around for a while, his lodging had been downgraded to a motel near Maggie Barlow's home, which wasn't a problem. He'd stayed in far worse places than a run-down motel in backwoods New York. If he could sleep in the Afghan hills with only his borrowed horse for company, then he'd survive without room service. Except he had no intention of staying at the motel.

Keeping tabs on Little Miss Maggie's book required access. The closer the better. He'd sleep on the floor if he had to, but one way or the other he planned on talking his way into her home.

But not her bed. Manipulating their mutual attraction to distract her when the questions hit too close to the "no-fly" territory was one thing. But he'd never used sex as a weapon against a woman and he didn't plan to start now. If he went to bed with her again, it would be because they both wanted it.

"Chief Cross."

Hunter turned and saw Maggie waving to him from the driver's seat of a vintage black Mercedes convertible. His jaw tightened and the irritation he'd felt during her presentation this morning boiled to the surface.

Where was her Toyota? If he hadn't witnessed her shock firsthand when he'd entered the trailer-turned-conference-room, he might have wondered if she'd sought him out Saturday night. But no, she hadn't driven a Toyota just to catch one of her "cowboys" and lure him into bed. The Toyota must be the car she used to pick up her Saturday night flings. His fist tightened around the Marriott bag. Hell, she'd probably built a complete persona for her carefully planned orgasm quests. He'd bet she'd never set foot in an Olive Garden. A woman who drove a car like that could afford high-end cuisine.

He turned his irritation down to a simmer. Give him one week and he'd show her. She'd messed with the wrong Ranger.

Hunter nodded hello. "Ms. Barlow."

She gave him a smile, but it didn't touch her eyes, not like it had in his hotel room.

"Get in." Maggie leaned across the console of her super-sleek car and opened the passenger-side door. "Please. I'd like to take you for a cup of coffee if you have some time. Clear the air before we get down to business."

The woman was nothing if not direct. Years of flings had primed him to expect a woman to brush the uncomfortable under the rug, not come clean and say, *Hey, remember how I asked you for amazing sex Saturday? Well let's talk about that so we can both focus on my book.*

Hunter opened the rear passenger-side door and tossed his duffel in the backseat. He held up the Marriott bag. "Your shoes."

"Thanks."

He slid into her car, which cost more than his annual salary and then some. "So, coffee?"

"There's a place in town." Maggie put the car in gear, her eyes on the road. "They have great cinnamon buns."

Hunter shook his head. "I can't talk openly about our missions in a public setting. We're better off at your place."

"My home?" He could hear the surprise in her voice.

"Unless you want to meet in my motel room."

She sighed with what he guessed was frustration as she pulled out of West Point and turned onto the main road. "My place it is. For today. I'll find somewhere private, but more professional for us to meet tomorrow. Before we debate locations, we should discuss Saturday."

Hunter turned to study Maggie as she kept her gaze focused on the road. He glanced down at her hands, positioned at ten and two on the steering wheel. Her right pinky finger tapped the wheel. He found her anxiety oddly reassuring. He might not know everything about the wealthy writer in the ugly suit, but he could still read her nerves.

"I had a great time," he said.

"I did, too."

Hunter studied the side of her face. One blond curl had escaped her severe hairdo and he wanted to reach out and give it a tug, but he stopped himself. He didn't like her. He shouldn't want to touch her.

"But I meant it when I said it was a onetime thing," she continued. "I just got out of a relationship. And on Saturday, well, let's just say I needed to find a part of myself. Does that make sense?"

"A serious relationship?" He narrowed his eyes, his gaze still fixed on the errant curl. What had this guy done to her that sent her hunting for orgasms?

Maggie flexed her hands around the steering wheel. "We were engaged."

Hunter's eyebrows shot up. A broken engagement, a one-night stand—it sounded as if Miss Maggie had more issues with commitment than he did. At least he hadn't been just another Saturday night. Her innocence hadn't been an act. She'd never gone searching for sex in a Toyota before her trip to the car show. He found that thought reassuring.

Not that it was any of his business, but he couldn't stop himself from asking. "What happened with your ex?"

She hesitated. "Irreconcilable differences."

Hunter looked out at the road as Maggie took a sharp turn without slowing down. He'd bet his next paycheck there was more to her breakup. "So you decided to ask the first stranger you met for an orgasm?"

"It wasn't my idea. But I admit, I think it makes sense to keep my personal and work life separate." She turned down a pine tree–lined drive and sped through an opening between two stone pillars, one marked with a private sign.

"Not working so well for you?"

"No. Not really."

"Relax, Maggie. You don't have to worry that I'm here for a repeat of Saturday night." Not that he'd object if she offered. Every time he looked at her he remembered the way her skin tasted against his lips, how her body felt pressed up against him.

Hunter stared past the trees into the open fields, trying to push the erotic images out of his mind. "I take my work seriously," he added.

The car slowed to a stop in front of a three-story white house with green shutters. A white wraparound porch circled the first level with a set of gray stairs leading up to the double door. Hunter didn't know the first thing about architecture, but if he had to guess, he'd say the place had to be two hundred years old. Ancient, but perfectly maintained.

First the car, now the house—Hunter had a feeling this mission wouldn't be as easy as he'd anticipated. Everything about her suggested this was a woman accustomed to being in command. Her need to cede control Saturday night had been an aberration, not the norm for her, which left him with an uphill battle when it came to her book.

But that wasn't what left his lower body aching. Even if her book hadn't come between them, they never would have gotten beyond the sex-in-the-hotel-room stage. Not when Little Miss Maggie parked her hundred-thousand-dollar car in front of a two-hundred-year-old mansion and he couldn't even afford an apartment with street parking for his fifteen-year-old truck.

A one-night stand was one thing, but ask for a repeat performance and a woman like her would expect things he couldn't provide. In his book, money and commitment went hand in hand. And right now, he couldn't afford either.

7

SHUFFLING THROUGH THE papers on her desk, Maggie replayed their conversation from the car over and over in her mind. Had he forgiven her for walking out on him? He hadn't been overly friendly, but she got the sense he meant it when he said his job took priority. At least, she hoped he did.

She unearthed her blue spiral notebook and scooped up her laptop, annoyed that he'd insisted on meeting in her home. She didn't want him calling the shots. Saturday night she'd followed his orders, but when it came to her book, she was in charge.

She walked back down the hall. Meeting here wasn't only a bad idea because he'd suggested it. People, men in particular, took one look at her grandfather's mansion and made assumptions about her. Some assumed her work was merely an amusing diversion, while others believed everything in her life came easy. No one guessed at the hard work it had taken to keep her family home and how the fear of failing, of losing the one stable place in her life, had left her determined to keep control. One wrong move would mean she'd failed her responsibilities.

Maggie made her way to the screened porch, pausing

with her hand on the doorknob when she spotted Hunter. She'd seen the man naked and still the sight of him lounging on her patio—his fingers laced behind his head, his biceps flexed and his worn black boots resting on her grandfather's ottoman—sent a thrill to parts of her body best forgotten while she worked. His toned arms shouted *touch me, squeeze me, caress me*. Even in profile, his face hinted at pleasure—those lips that had licked and kissed her into paradise, those George Clooney eyes.

But this wasn't the relaxed pose of a man waiting for a woman. Hunter looked like a lion surrounded by wicker. Large. Imposing. Ready to spring up from his sprawled position and pounce on his prey—her.

Maggie's grip tightened on her laptop and notebook, but she didn't look away. Hands down, the man was gorgeous. But if he thought he could run roughshod over her with his sex appeal, he was sorely mistaken. Now was not the time to let him call the shots.

Maggie stepped onto the porch, her fingers drumming against her laptop. Hunter turned to her and she met his brown bedroom eyes. Maybe it was her imagination, but the look in there hinted at take-me-now need. His gaze seemed to say *I know your fantasies, your secrets, your vulnerabilities*.

"Maggie?"

The sound of his voice went right to her nipples, driving them into tight peaks. He might as well have reached across the room and touched her breasts. Either this man was trying to distract her with sex or the natural chemistry she'd felt Saturday night had pushed her right to the edge—or maybe it was a disastrous combination of the two.

Hunter offered her another seductive smile and Maggie knew it was a trick. Maybe he'd forgiven her for walking

out Saturday night, but Chief Hunter Cross still had something up his sleeve.

She looked over his head to the open fields and counted
to ten. This was her interview. She was in charge here.
Then she turned her gaze back to him, careful not to look
straight at him.

"I have my notes, so if you're ready, I'd like to start."
Thankfully, she sounded like a professional and not a
turned-on mess. Still on edge, she sat on the chair across
from his and set her laptop down on the table. "Can I offer
you tea? Cookies? Coffee?"

"Maybe later." His sexy smile faded. "First, I need to
set the record straight on one thing. I'm not a cowboy and
neither are my teammates. I rode a horse because it was my
job. While I was there, I didn't discharge my weapon until
we rode out to rescue those women. Not even to slaughter
a goat for dinner when we ran out of MREs during our
ride." He paused. "Ready-made meals."

"I know what they are." Maggie scribbled a note about
the goat and looked up at him. This time, when she peered
into his eyes, it wasn't about sex. The thrill of her job—
finding a story and putting it together, discovering new
facts—pushed aside her desire. "You want me to change
the title of my book."

Hunter nodded.

"Because you don't think of yourself as a cowboy,"
she said.

"It's an insult to my team." He leaned forward, resting
his forearms on his knees. "If you start your interviews
tossing out the word *cowboy* left and right like you did
this morning, you're not going to get much out of them."

"Point taken, and we'll circle back to the title of my
book. I'm more interested in when I can arrange to speak

with your teammates. Would Thursday work? I can book flights today—"

"Afraid not." Hunter shook his head and leaned back in his chair. "You need to sit down with Connor, Jed and Mike. I took the liberty of checking their schedules and all of them are on a training mission until Friday. You'll have to interview them this weekend. They ship out again on Monday."

"This weekend for Connor, Jed and Mike," she said. "What about the others? I thought there were six of you."

"That's right. But let's not get ahead of ourselves. I thought we were going to chat about us first and save the interviews for later."

Maggie frowned. "I think we said everything that needed to be said in the car."

Hunter raised his arms and laced his fingers behind his head, flexing his biceps. "You really are an all work or all play kind of girl, aren't you?"

No, she wasn't. That was part of the problem. Her mind might be turned to work mode, but right now, at this moment, her body was reacting to the sight of his powerful arms.

"Back to the schedule," she said, pretending to study her computer screen.

"If you insist." He dropped his arms down. "Riley, our former team leader, left the army after our last mission. He lives about forty-five minutes north of here." Hunter smiled. "He was with me at the car show before you approached."

Thank God she'd waited until his friend left. Maggie did her best to appear unaffected by his reference to Saturday, while inside her stomach gave a little flip. "Great, when can I sit down with him?"

"I'll give him a call and let you know," he said.

"And the sixth member of your team?"

Hunter hesitated for the first time since she'd sat down. "He's taking some R & R. It might be a while before I can track him down."

She needed firsthand accounts of the Rangers' ride, but she might not have to speak with all six members of the team. Still, something about Hunter's response didn't sit right with her. "Were you close with your teammates?"

"Like brothers."

"Did you always deploy together?" she asked, her fingers moving over the keyboard.

"No. This was the only time I'd worked with Connor. He completed Ranger school weeks before we deployed."

"Then why send him? Could he ride better than the other Rangers?"

"First, he's a computer geek and we needed someone who knew our equipment backward and forward. And second, no one knew about the horses until we met up with our Afghan contact."

"Did you think it was a trick? The horses? Some military divisions refuse to work with the Afghans after so many of them have turned around and shot the American soldiers sent in to train them."

"We're not most soldiers."

"You didn't answer the question," Maggie fired back.

"There was always a risk that it was a trick. Our contact could have led us into an ambush. But our commanding officers decided the mission—rescuing those American women—was worth taking the risk."

Maggie typed furiously as he spoke, and then paused. "I still don't understand how you didn't know about the horses. Someone had been in touch with this local warlord? He knew you were coming?"

Hunter nodded. "He reached out to us. He offered to

lead us to where the aid workers were being held. No one thought to ask about the mode of transportation. We were expecting trucks and he arrived with horses. In hindsight, someone should have made the connection. The gifts our friend requested included vodka and oats."

Maggie leaned forward in her chair. "Oats?"

He let out a laugh, shaking his head. "Yeah, oats. One of the bags opened up when the cargo ship dropped us. I guess the guys prepping our mission assumed the Afghans liked oatmeal."

Maggie smiled, feeling some of the tension in her body ease. He'd relaxed and stopped fighting for control, at least for the time being. She watched him sit back in the chair. He rolled his shoulder, the injured one, as if it pained him. She frowned. "You were shot on this mission, correct?"

Again he hesitated. "Yes."

"What happened?" In her mind, she pictured him bleeding while riding a galloping horse through the Afghan mountains.

"That's classified."

Maggie raised an eyebrow. "I have security clearance." She'd fought long and hard to get it for her research.

"Classified and personal," he said.

The tension between them was palpable, but no longer entirely sexual. The writer in her told her she was on to something.

"Hello? Maggie?" Olivia's voice shattered the tension.

What was Olivia doing here? And why had she chosen the worst possible time to interrupt? Maggie felt a brief moment of panic as if she'd been caught doing something naughty.

"Maggs?" Olivia called a second time.

But there was no reason to be alarmed. Maggie was working. Nothing improper about that. Still, she wasn't ready to explain Hunter's presence to her best friend. Not that she had a choice now. She stood, notebook in hand, and called out, "On the porch."

Olivia marched through the door wearing a hot-pink-and-black print dress and black high-heeled boots. She froze when she saw Hunter and turned to Maggie.

"We need to work on your definition of a one-night stand."

Tell me about it, she thought. "Liv, meet Chief Hunter Cross."

Olivia raised an eyebrow. "We've met."

Out of the corner of her eye, Maggie saw Hunter stand, hook his fingers through the loops in the front of his jeans and smile at Olivia. "Good to see you again."

"Hunter is my army liaison. We were just starting our first interview."

"Uh-huh." Olivia smiled at her. "I knew I'd interrupted something."

"Wait here," Maggie said to Hunter. She picked up her pen and laptop and then turned to Olivia, determined to fix this situation so she could get back to her interview. "You. Come with me."

She led Olivia into the kitchen, dumping her laptop on the marble-topped kitchen island.

"What are you doing here?" she whispered. Brick walls and glass windows separated the porch from the kitchen, but she wasn't taking any chances. She would have dragged Olivia to her study, but she didn't want to let Hunter out of her sight for too long. After the way he'd tried to distract her on the porch, she suspected he might take himself on a guided tour—straight to her bedroom.

"What am *I* doing here? Why is *he* here?" Olivia demanded, hands on her hips.

"I need him here. For work. Believe me, I'd rather have

anyone else." Like a Ranger who didn't make her think about sex. "But he's what they gave me."

"Lucky you."

"Liv, he's not the same man. The man I met Saturday night was a gentleman. *That* man is dangerous."

"But in a good way." Olivia's attention turned from the window back to Maggie. "Unlike your scumbag ex."

"Derrick?" What did he have to do with anything? She'd given him back the ring. It was over.

"He called me this morning at the gallery."

"Derrick called you at work?" Needing to do something, Maggie walked over to the fridge. Her world was usually orderly and predictable, but today? The surprises just kept coming. She was beginning to wonder if this day would ever end. Her one-night fling stood on her porch, her ex-fiancé had called her best friend at work and it wasn't even lunchtime yet.

"He wants you back." Olivia smiled, a wide grin reminiscent of the Cheshire cat from *Alice in Wonderland.* Oh, no, this couldn't be good.

"Olivia, what did you do?"

"I told him to rot in hell. And I may have hinted that you'd moved on. Of course, if I'd known you'd decided to keep your one-night stand until Monday—"

"Enough, Liv. How'd Derrick take that?" Derrick had always been the sensible type. Maggie couldn't imagine him putting up a fight to keep her, not when he hadn't really wanted her in the first place.

"Not good. He said he had to see you himself."

"He's coming up from the city?" No, this couldn't be happening. Not now. She had her book to write, a blog to build and her army liaison to manage. Maggie glanced out at the porch. Hunter was still there. And watching her through the glass window with interest.

She opened the fridge and pulled out three beers, then glanced at the kitchen clock. Five till noon. Close enough. She set two bottles on the counter and twisted off the top of the third. She'd bought the beer for one of Derrick's visits and had forgotten about it until now. But if there was ever a reason to have a drink in the middle of the day, it was when your cheating ex threatened to drop by for a visit. Plus, she needed to keep Hunter occupied.

"Wait here, Liv."

Maggie marched onto the porch and thrust the beer at Hunter, who, for the first time since he'd entered her home, looked off balance.

"For while you wait," she said. "This shouldn't take long."

"Isn't it a little early?" he asked.

"It's been a long day."

She retreated to the kitchen and sank onto a barstool. Removing the top of her beer, she took a sip, the wheels turning in her head.

"I don't suppose you want to have a sleepover tonight?" Maggie asked.

Olivia set her bottle down on the counter. "Why would you need me when you have Mr. Army Ranger? He'll scare Derrick away."

"Yeah, but who will keep Hunter away?"

"You wanted access to the army rangers. Now you have it…if you can convince him to stay the night."

"He can't stay here. He's trying to use his sex appeal to take charge of my interviews."

Olivia snorted. "You, out of control? I can't picture it, and I've known you since the second grade."

Oh, it had happened. And part of the problem was Maggie could "picture it."

"Is it working?" Olivia asked.

"It's distracting. But I'll manage. As long as I keep our relationship strictly professional, which means he can't stay here, Liv. I'll have to deal with Derrick on my own. If he even bothers to show up."

"You're sure? Because I need to get back to the gallery and get ready for tonight's show."

"I'm sure." She forced a smile. "Haven't I always taken care of myself?"

Maggie took a long drink as the kitchen door swung closed behind Olivia. Staying in control, tackling responsibilities alone—it was the only way she knew to survive. Dealing with Derrick would be nothing compared to what she'd already handled. She didn't need an army ranger decoy.

8

HUNTER PARKED HIS rental car, a basic Ford that looked as out of place as he felt beside Maggie's Mercedes, and checked his watch. Three minutes till seven. Maggie had asked him to be back by six for their dinner session, but he had every intention of starting his interview on the late side.

She'd probably try to send him packing, even if they talked until midnight. But if he drank one too many? She'd have to let him crash on the couch. He could mention the pain meds he was supposed to be taking and had refused. He'd learned a thing or two about addiction from his sister. He had no intention of heading down that path.

Thunder rolled in the distance as he opened his car door. He looked up and saw the storm clouds moving in. Taking his time, he retrieved the bottle of red wine he'd picked up in town and locked the car, and then at precisely 1900 hours, he walked up the front steps and rang the bell.

Maggie opened the door, motioning for him to enter. "You're late."

"I had a few things to take care of," he lied. He'd spent the past few hours driving around town looking for a decent but affordable wine store. He held out the Chianti he'd selected from the sale basket. "I picked up a red. The guy at the store recommended it."

"Thanks," she said, accepting the bottle. Judging from her expression, his gesture had caught her off guard. She probably figured she'd drawn the line in the sand earlier. This was work, not a social event. But her manners kept her from refusing his gift.

Maggie closed the door and led the way down the hall. "Dinner might be cold by now, but there's a lot of it. I hope you're hungry."

His stomach grumbled. When was the last time he'd eaten? Breakfast? The beer around noon didn't count.

"I'll take that as a yes." She pushed through the swinging door. "I hope you don't mind eating in the kitchen. I've turned the dining room into a work space."

"Nope." Hunter pulled out a wooden chair with a green seat cushion from the table by the window and watched Maggie remove the take-out containers from a brown paper bag.

She'd changed out of the shapeless gray suit she'd worn to their morning meeting and into loose-fitting black sweats. In his experience, a woman wore form-fitting workout clothes to emphasize the shape of her butt. Not Maggie Barlow. Her pants hung from her waist, hiding the curves he remembered from Saturday night.

But her zipped-up black sweatshirt molded to her full breasts, gaping open at the neck to reveal the white straps of her tank top and, on her left shoulder, a beige bra strap.

He studied that strap, allowing his gaze to drift down to her chest. Hands down, he preferred her braless. Not that his preferences mattered much now. He'd only let his eyes wander to unsettle her so she'd forget her questions.

Uh-huh. And the horse he'd ridden through hostile territory had gone on to win the Kentucky Derby.

"Which one do you want?" It didn't sound as though Maggie had noticed his intense focus on her body.

"Hmm?"

"Rigatoni with sausage and peas, or lasagna? I ordered the whole wheat with veggies for myself, but you're welcome to part of it."

"Lasagna." What happened to the Maggie who craved linguine Alfredo? Or was that only on Saturdays?

She pushed a container in front of him, opened the Chianti and poured him a glass before she claimed the chair across from him. She'd placed a legal pad and pen beside her, but no computer. He had a hunch Miss Maggie was trying to make him comfortable. Like this wasn't a real interview. Yeah, right. Anything he said over pasta could end up in print.

"Do you mind if I ask you a few questions while we eat?"

Hunter smiled. "Can I ask you something first?"

The corners of her mouth dipped into a frown. "Sure."

"Why this mission? And don't tell me it's because people liked the picture in the paper."

Maggie set down her fork. "Honestly, that's part of it. I need to write a bestseller and people are interested in your ride. But why do I think it's important? A lot of people would argue this is the way modern warfare should be fought."

"On horseback?"

"With small teams of highly trained soldiers going in to work alongside the good guys living in the area, the ones who have a vested interest in removing the enemy. Smaller teams also mean less loss of life." She smiled. "And it certainly worked for the SEALs who took on bin Laden. Look at what a small group of men and a dog accomplished."

And look at how much press they got for it, Hunter thought.

"My turn to ask the questions." She picked up her pen.

"I have one more," he said. The storm had kicked into full gear now. Rain pounded against the window and thunder echoed in the nearby hills. "How did you become an expert on the military?"

Maggie raised an eyebrow. "You want my credentials?"

"Something like that."

"I started studying the armed forces in high school," she said. "My dad was a Ranger, which you probably knew."

Hunter nodded. He'd read the briefing materials.

"He didn't handle the end of his military career well. He drank," she said flatly. "I was young when he first came home, but I'd already lost my mother. My grandfather passed away shortly after my dad's return. It was just the two of us, and he seemed like a different person. It never got better."

"You became the adult. You took care of him. And the house." He could feel the tension between them heating up. Not the push and pull over who asked the questions. The tension he felt in his body had everything to do with reaching out and touching the woman who was beginning to look a lot more like the Maggie he'd met Saturday night—brazen and bold, and wise beyond her years in so many ways, but innocent in others.

Maggie stared down into her glass. "I did. I paid the bills and hired a housekeeper to buy the groceries and cook. I was probably the only ten-year-old who could balance a checkbook and research treatment options for alcoholics. Not that my father ever agreed to go."

"That's a lot for a kid." He drained his wineglass and helped himself to a refill. He knew all about researching treatment options. It was a hell of a responsibility for someone in grade school. "When did your dad pass away?"

"Two years ago." She pushed the pasta around in her take-out container with her fork. "His liver finally went."

Her entire adult life and most of her childhood had been spent caring for her father. Talk about commitment to family. His sacrifices for his sister paled in comparison. "And you started researching the military to better understand your father?"

"And grandfather. He always spoke of the years he served in the army with pride, like it was his greatest accomplishment. There's something inspiring about the men and women who put their country first, risking their lives in war zones. I think a lot of people look at the military as a unit, and some are quick to criticize our armed forces. They forget about the individuals wearing the uniforms."

Hunter frowned. "The media plays a role in that. If they'd stop publicizing some stupid mistakes made by one or two soldiers, the army would have a better image."

"Agreed," she said. "And I'd like to think my book can help change that image by providing an in-depth look at your heroic mission."

She didn't sound intent on revealing his teammate's mistake. But with Maggie, things weren't always as they appeared. One look at this house and he'd made assumptions. She had money, yes, but judging from what little he'd learned of her childhood, she was still struggling for stability.

"So you want to write the feel-good military book of the year," he said.

"I guess you could say that. I prefer to think of it as a positive and honest look at a successful mission." She pushed her plate aside and reached for her pen. "My turn to ask the questions."

Yeah, that wasn't going to happen. His gaze drifted to the porch as he refilled his glass. For what? The third time? Or was it the fourth? He'd stopped counting. He had a high tolerance for alcohol, but downing wine this fast was starting to get to him.

Miss Maggie had noticed. As the daughter of an alcoholic she was probably programmed to count drinks. She drew the bottle closer to her side of the table, out of his reach.

"How about we move this conversation to the porch now that the brunt of the storm has passed?" Hunter picked up his wineglass and headed for the door. "Get some fresh air—the rain has almost stopped."

"All right, then. Porch it is," she said, scooping up her notepad. "But that won't stop the questions."

Hunter walked out onto the porch and set his glass on the side table. He turned to face her. Determined from head to toe, that was his Maggie. Only she wasn't his.

Hunter frowned as his gaze fell from the pit-bull expression on her face to her shoulders. There it was. The beige bra strap. Taunting him, teasing him. He wanted her, but he knew he shouldn't act on those feelings. He'd come here tonight with every intention of talking his way into an overnight invitation. On her couch. Anything else would be unprofessional. He knew better than to give in to desire while working an op. But his missions usually involved men with guns, not sexy professors.

Maggie closed the door behind her, preventing the warm, humid air from slipping into the air-conditioned house. She waved to the chairs with her notepad. "Would you like to sit?"

Lips pursed, gaze focused, her left hand clutching her pen like a weapon—it was a textbook red light, don't-touch-me look. But he took a step forward anyway. Maybe it was that bra strap or maybe it was the wine. Either way something had short-circuited his brain, allowing the part of his body below his belt to call the shots. One kiss— what could it hurt?

"I've been thinking about what we discussed in the car earlier," he said. "About Saturday being a one-time thing." Wrapping his hand around her hip, he pulled her to him. His other hand pried the notebook out of her grasp, tossing it on a nearby chair. Then he stole her pen. "Thing is, I want a repeat performance."

Maggie pressed her hands against his chest. "I think you've had too much to drink."

"Maybe." He ran his free hand up and down the soft curve of her body. "But that doesn't change the fact that I want you, Maggie."

It was the God's honest truth. His hands itched to tease her breasts and he didn't want to stop there.

"I don't think this is a good idea." She tried to step out of his grasp, but her body didn't put any real effort into it. In her mind, she might be ticking off all the reasons they shouldn't do this, but he knew her body wanted him. Her fingers burrowed into his shirt even as the rest of her pulled away.

But he couldn't take the chance her brain would win the battle. "How about a kiss for a question? One little kiss? What could it hurt?"

"A kiss—"

He cut her off, capturing her mouth with his. He kissed her hard, his tongue running over her lips, demanding entrance. It was the Marriott elevator all over again. She wanted to let go and abandon herself to him. He could feel it in the way her hips swayed toward him and then pulled back. But this time, it wasn't the fear of discovery that held her back. It was those damn thoughts and doubts rushing through her mind.

He wanted to make her forget her fears and lose herself in his kiss. Snaking one arm around her back, holding her close, he worked his free hand under her shirt until he felt bare skin. Palm flat against her taut stomach, his fingers drifted upward, reaching for her bra. Edging his hand underneath the fabric-covered wire, he didn't stop until the full weight of her breast rested in his palm. He squeezed then brushed his hand back and forth over her taut nipple, teasing, touching, demanding, waiting for the moment her desire pushed aside her fears and she gave in to the sensations.

It didn't take long. Maggie melted into his touch and he doubted she remembered his offer to answer a question in exchange for their kiss, which suited him just fine. He had no intention of getting to the Q & A part of their little game.

Driving his tongue into her mouth, Hunter withdrew his hand from under her shirt and let go of her waist. Before she could back away, he wrapped his hands around the sides of her head, massaging his fingers into her scalp as he kissed her. Holding her still, he thrust his tongue forward and back against hers, wishing it was another part of his anatomy.

"Christ, Maggie, I want you," he muttered, their lips still touching, his fingers buried in her hair. "I want to make you lose control."

MAGGIE WENT FROM pliant to stiff as a board in a heartbeat. The panic she'd felt in his hotel room Saturday night returned in a rush. Oh, God. Oh, God. What was she doing? Placing her hands on his chest, she pushed him away.

"We can't do this," she said, meeting his gaze, the words

coming out in a rush. "We're working together. I need to interview you in the morning. It wouldn't be professional."

"I hate to admit it, but you're right," he said, but he didn't move away.

"I think you should go." She let her hand fall from his chest as she stepped back. "We'll keep our interviews to the daylight hours from now on." Still trembling from the wild mix of lust and alarm, she bent over to pick up her discarded notebook.

"I'm afraid I've had too much wine to drive tonight," he admitted. "Any chance I could crash on your couch?"

Her head snapped up, her eyes meeting his somewhat sheepish gaze. She couldn't let him sleep here. This man tested the limits of her self-control. He made her forget herself and that couldn't happen again.

"I'll call you a cab," she said quickly, moving to the door.

"No, don't worry about it." He shook his head, his voice slightly slurred. "I'm sure I'll be fine after a glass of water. It's probably more of a reaction to the pain pill I took earlier for my shoulder. They sometimes leave me a little light-headed. If I sit down for a few minutes and have something to drink, I'll be okay to hit the road."

"Pain pill," she repeated as alarm bells went off in her head.

"Might also be the reason I couldn't keep my hands off you," he added, his eyes dropping to her chest. "Although I suspect that has more to do with you than the wine."

She crossed her arms in front of her. Alcohol and pain pills. Heaven help her, he had more in common with her father than she'd initially suspected.

Despite what had just happened, she'd never let anyone, not even her worst enemy, drive while intoxicated. She'd spent too many sleepless nights wondering if her father would risk his life behind the wheel or call a cab to get home from the bar. She could let Hunter crash here for one night. It might not be professional, or good for her sanity, but then neither was kissing him on the porch, and she couldn't blame her lapse in judgment on the wine.

"You can stay in the downstairs guest room. But only for tonight."

Hunter smiled his relief. "Great. You won't even know I'm here. I promise."

Somehow she doubted that. His presence seemed to drift through the walls, filling the house. "Let me get my notes and I'll show you to your room."

Maggie heard a faint vibrating noise as she retrieved her notepad from the chair. She looked back at Hunter and saw him pull his phone from his pocket.

He frowned and his hazy I'm-too-drunk-to-drive look vanished. "I need to take this. If you'll excuse me."

"Of course," she said in her best all-business tone. "You can use my study. First door on the left. I'll wait for you in the kitchen."

"Thanks."

Maggie followed him inside, watching as he pressed a button and raised the phone to his ear. Judging from his serious expression, she guessed his commanding officer or someone from his team was on the other line.

"Sierra?" he said before the kitchen door swung shut behind him.

Or maybe not. Whoever it was, she was grateful for the interruption.

Maggie set her notebook on the island and scanned her list of unanswered questions. But her mind refused to focus. What had happened on the porch had left her seriously shaken. Out of control, but not in the way that led to orgasms.

She felt something for him. Common sense told her she wasn't falling in love with him. How could she? She'd only known the man a matter of days, and she had a sneaking suspicion he'd only kissed her tonight to stop her from asking questions. He'd gone from drunk to serious in a matter of seconds when he'd received that call. She doubted alcohol had been the driving factor behind his little seduction. It was just one more way for him to gain the upper hand.

But whatever Hunter's reasons, they didn't change the fact that she felt something. Wild, crazy lust. And from where she was standing now, lust seemed just as dangerous as handing over her heart.

Maggie closed her notebook and headed for the hallway. Tomorrow she'd refocus on interviewing Hunter. They could start over breakfast. She pushed through the swinging door and stepped into the hall to prepare the guest room.

"Sierra, you're not listening to me." Hunter's voice slipped into the hall.

Maggie stilled. Who was Sierra?

Deciding the guest bedroom could wait, she tiptoed up to her study door and pressed her ear against the wood.

"No, Sierra. I want you to stay there." Hunter sounded frustrated and he wasn't bothering to keep his voice down. "Last time you left, you almost died. You're ready to leave when the doctors say you're ready. Not a moment before. Is that clear?"

There was a brief pause. "I'll find a way to get the money. Don't worry about that. How much more do you need?"

What did this mysterious woman need money for?

"Okay. That's doable." His tone was resigned. "When do you need it?"

Another pause.

"Okay. Let them know I'll send a check."

Hunter was quiet for a minute.

"No, I'm not at the base, but your doctors have my address. I emailed it to them this afternoon. Just do me a favor and don't leave, okay? You need to be there. Can you promise me you'll stay?" Silence. And then, "I'm going to hold you to that."

She heard footsteps and rushed away from the door and down the hall to the front stairs. The writer in her wanted to pepper him with questions. Who was this woman? What did she mean to him? Was she his girlfriend? He had referenced doctors on the phone. Maybe she was someone he'd met while recovering from his gunshot wound?

A sinking feeling settled in her gut and she took the stairs two at a time. From the sound of their conversation, Sierra wasn't a casual acquaintance. What if Hunter was another cheating bastard?

No. Not possible. Hunter Cross might be a controlling army ranger today, but on Saturday night, he'd been a gentleman.

Still, that didn't explain Sierra.

Maggie reached the second floor and paused. She had to confront him. But she'd wait until tomorrow. He could find his way to the guest room or crash on the couch, but after all that had happened this evening, she needed a break from the man who threatened to send her life—her career, her emotions, everything—out of control.

9

HUNTER SANK INTO the desk chair and closed his eyes. In front of him sat Maggie's computer. Now would be the perfect time to do a little recon, maybe take a peek at the notes she'd typed up and see how much she knew about the snafu that had left him with a bullet in his shoulder. But he couldn't take his mind off his conversation with Sierra.

How could she walk away from rehab when only a few months ago she'd nearly died from an overdose? She'd been damn lucky he'd been stateside when her boyfriend of the week had called him to say Sierra was unconscious. He'd rushed over to his sister's apartment and found her alone. The bastard boyfriend hadn't even waited around for him to show up and take her to the hospital.

The helpless fear he'd experienced sitting at her bedside came rushing back, and he pushed it away. He didn't do helpless. Sierra needed to stay in rehab. Whatever it took, he'd do it.

Hunter drew a deep breath, but the air inside Maggie's study felt hot and stifling. Fresh air. That's what he needed now. A long walk. Then when he got back to the house, after Maggie had fallen asleep, he could snoop around her computer and focus on the job he was getting paid to do before crashing in her guest room.

He stood and left the study, pocketing his phone. After poking his head into the kitchen and finding it empty, he went to the base of the stairs. "Maggie?"

"Yes?" She sounded distant. Hell, in this house she could be half a mile away. But then he heard footsteps and a second later she appeared at the top of the stairs. She offered a forced smile. Her hair hung loose, the soft curls grazing her shoulders. Had she been in bed? His body instantly responded, while his mind silently chastised him. *Don't go there.*

"I'm going out for a walk," he called up to her. "I need some fresh air. Those pain pills...they're really getting to me. No need to wait up."

Maggie nodded. "Okay. The guest room is the first door on the right past the living room. The sheets on the bed should be clean. I didn't get a chance to check them, but—"

"Any sheets work for me. I won't be long. And I won't disturb you when I come back in. Good night."

He turned toward the front door.

"Oh, and Hunter?" she called after him.

Hand on the knob, he looked back up the stairs. Maggie bit her lip as if she wasn't sure she should have called him back.

"Please lock up when you come inside."

"Will do." He watched her disappear down the dark hall, wondering if she was just tired or disappointed with their first day of interviews. She'd probably hoped he'd spill his guts over dinner. Not going to happen, tonight or any other night. Talking to Sierra had served as a wake-up call. He needed to follow his orders and get his pay raise. His sister's recovery and her future hung in the balance. This wasn't just about him. Sierra needed him.

He stepped out into the warm summer night and checked his watch. Nearly 2100 hours and the sun still hovered above the horizon. A cool breeze drifted past and he decided to head into the light wind. He had a hunch he'd find the Hudson River beyond Maggie's manicured fields.

As he walked, he ran through the numbers in his head. His checking account currently held about two thousand, and Sierra needed every penny to pay for another month in rehab. If he didn't spend a dime between now and his next paycheck, he could swing it. Barely. But if the doctors demanded Sierra stay at the clinic for another month? He'd better be back on active duty. He needed the extra parachute duty pay. And to earn that, he had to complete parachute jumps even if his shoulder protested.

Hunter picked up the pace, trying to burn off his frustration with movement. Rehab better work this time. If Sierra started using again when she got out, he didn't know what he'd do. Come up with the money somehow.

He heard the sound of the water before he saw the riverbank. In the fading light, he spotted a few boats floating downstream. A fence stood about fifty paces away and then the hill dropped off sharply. Railroad tracks crossed below, running parallel to the river. With a little more light, or his night vision equipment, he'd be able to see across to the other side. But tonight, the moon didn't shine brightly enough to make out anything beyond the center of the Hudson.

Not even with the extra couple of hundred a month in jump pay could he ever dream of living in a place like this. Waterfront property would forever be out of his reach unless he wanted to live by a swamp—or he hooked up long-term with a woman like Maggie.

Not going to happen, he thought, closing his eyes. The Rangers were more than a job; they were his life. And it was a life that didn't have a place for a relationship with Little Miss Maggie, at least not the boyfriend/girlfriend kind.

Turning away from the river, Hunter stared at the massive brick house in the distance. It didn't matter who Maggie was to him or how much he wanted to see her naked again. He needed to put an end to this mission and get back to his life. Sierra needed him. His team needed him. And Maggie didn't. She'd made that perfectly clear when she'd walked out Saturday night. She'd been looking for a way to expand her sexual horizons and get over her ex.

Part of him wanted to be her go-to guy for sexual fantasies. What they'd done Saturday night had been the tip of the iceberg. Seeing her at work and learning what she'd gone through as a child, he had a better understanding of why she wanted to relinquish her control in the bedroom. He wanted to be the one who set her free from her responsibilities. Hell, he wanted to be the guy who bound her to the bedpost and gave her orgasm after sweet orgasm.

But he couldn't do that. Not while they were working together.

Hunter shook his head and headed for the house. It was time to get to work. He quickly retraced his steps and slipped in the main entrance, turning the lock behind him. Moving as silently as an intruder just in case Maggie hadn't fallen asleep yet, Hunter made his way down the hall to her study. He opened the door and slipped into the dark, empty room. Without turning on a light, he crossed to the desk and slid into the chair.

Feeling like a snake even though he'd completed similar missions in the past, he opened her laptop. Then he withdrew his phone and dialed.

"Connor." His teammate, the computer specialist, answered after the first ring.

"Hey, man, you busy?" Hunter pressed the power button and waited for the computer to come to life.

"Hunter. Good to hear from you. You recovered yet? I haven't seen you around the base."

"I'm back, but working on something for the colonel, and I need your skills." The screen lit up, and as he'd suspected, it asked for a password. "How do I hack into a password-protected computer?"

"Start with guessing."

Hunter came up blank. Maggie didn't have a living pet as far as he could tell and he didn't know enough about her to come up with anything else. He doubted she'd use *linguine Alfredo* or the color *green* for her password.

"I've got nothing," he said.

"Okay, your phone has a SIM card in it. You still have that USB drive I gave you on your keychain?"

"Yeah." He reached for a piece of paper and a pen. Connor walked him through the steps and he wrote everything down.

"Now hang up and download the program I just sent to your SIM, pop it into the USB drive and then plug that into the computer."

Hunter followed his teammate's instructions, keeping one ear out for any sounds in the hall. Five minutes later, he was in. He called Connor back. "Got it. Thanks, man. I owe you a beer when I get back."

"Planning on coming back soon? We're gonna miss your sorry ass on this week's training op."

"I'll be back this weekend. I need you and some of the other guys to sit down for an interview with a professor who's writing a book about us."

"No shit," Connor said. "She wants to talk to all of us?"

"Yeah. Get different sides of the story."

"She's not some journalist trying to make us look like a

bunch of fools, is she? Logan would hate to have the whole world know about that little clusterfuck."

"Don't worry about it," Hunter said. "I've got her under control. You just have to spread the word to keep your mouth shut if she asks about how I got shot."

"Not a problem. I'll tell Jed and Mike," Connor replied. "Shoot me a text or give a shout if you need more help."

Hunter hung up the phone and focused on the program open in front of him. From the looks of it, Miss Maggie had started work on her blog. The header across the top featured the picture of his team on horseback, their faces mostly covered with handkerchiefs. Below the picture ran the headline: Meet America's Cowboy Heroes.

He scrolled down. The rest of the page was blank. No entries yet. He minimized the window and scanned her desktop until a document labeled Promotion Deadlines caught his attention. Opening the file, he found a list of dates, including this coming Sunday. It read: *Launch blog. Publisher eager to get it up and running.*

Hunter closed the computer, careful to shut it down first. Glancing at his watch, he saw the digital numbers change to midnight. It was officially Tuesday. He had five days to convince her to change the title of her blog. He knew the colonel would prefer he shut the entire thing down, but knowing Maggie, she'd dig in her heels. Controlling the content—and the author—was his best option.

10

BUZZ. BUZZ.

What was that noise? Maggie opened her eyes, then quickly closed them to block out the sunlight pouring in through the uncovered windows. She'd been so exhausted last night she'd forgotten to pull the curtains when she'd fallen into bed. Turning away from the light, she opened one eye to look at her alarm clock. Six in the morning.

Buzz. Buzz.

The doorbell. Someone was at her front door. Groggily, she pushed back the covers and stood, sliding her feet into her waiting slippers. Shuffling to the door, she removed her gray robe from the hook and wrapped it around her white tank and gray yoga pants. Her hair was probably sticking out in a million directions, but right now she didn't care. She wanted to figure out who was at her door and get a cup of coffee, not necessarily in that order. She stumbled out of her room and made her way down the front stairs.

Maggie froze on the bottom step. Hunter, her self-invited houseguest, was already at the door, fully dressed in jeans and a black T-shirt as if he'd been up for hours. For all she knew about his morning habits, maybe he woke with the sun. She watched him peer through the peephole.

"Are you expecting a delivery?" he asked.

"UPS is here?" Her brow furrowed. Why would the UPS man be on her doorstep now? She needed coffee. She'd never been able to think straight first thing in the morning without caffeine.

"Not UPS. Some guy with a box." He turned to her, frowning as the doorbell buzzed again. "Want me to send him away?"

"No, I—"

"Maggie?" She'd been about to say she could handle it when Derrick's voice interrupted.

"Oh, crap, I know him," she said, closing her eyes briefly. "Go ahead and let him in. Bring him into the kitchen. I need coffee."

"Yes, ma'am." He sounded more amused than put off at playing butler.

Resigned to an awkward early morning conversation with her ex, Maggie walked past Hunter with as much dignity as she could muster in her robe and slippers. Of course, Derrick would pleasantly knock on her door when she looked and felt her worst. Morning. The man was a self-centered fool. A smart, caring person would never try to woo her before coffee. Or think he had a chance at winning her back after she'd caught him with his pants down.

She pushed through the swinging door leading to the kitchen, and the smell hit her. Coffee. Freshly brewed, hot and steaming. Maggie smiled. Hunter must have made it at whatever ungodly hour he'd risen. Apparently, not all morning people were brainless twits. Just Derrick.

"Good morning, Maggie." Derrick ambled into the kitchen, set the box on the counter and leaned over to kiss her. She turned her mouth away and let him peck her cheek before stepping away. Hunter walked in just in time to witness the kiss. He raised an eyebrow. Maggie mouthed thank you for the coffee over her ex-fiancé's shoulder. Her professional self might not want Hunter here, but since he'd insisted on staying, she had every intention of using him to send Derrick away for good.

"I brought you muffins," Derrick said. "Your favorite. Low-fat vanilla pear from that bakery you like in the city."

Low fat had never been her favorite. She preferred cinnamon buns dripping with sugary frosting. She'd switched to reduced-calorie food after she'd accepted his proposal two months ago. Apparently his memory didn't go back that far. And if he'd brought them from Manhattan, that meant he'd picked them up yesterday. Low fat and stale, not exactly the way to a girl's heart.

Maggie sipped her coffee and studied Derrick. He'd shaved that morning, styled his blond hair into the usual side part that made him look like something out of a country club advertisement and put on a blue power suit.

"Meeting later?" she asked over the rim of her coffee, taking a sip before she bit out the words *with one of your students*.

"Yes, but I had to see you first after the way we left things last time." He glanced at Hunter, standing with his arms folded across his chest by the door. "I didn't realize you'd hired a bodyguard."

"I didn't." She plucked a muffin from the box and walked over to Hunter's side. "He's a friend. Derrick, this is Hunter. Hunter, meet Derrick." She looked up at Hunter, silently begging him to play along. "Muffin?"

Hunter smiled down at her. "Love one." He plucked the poor excuse for a breakfast treat from her hand and took a bite. "I can see why these are your favorite. Loads of flavor."

Maggie stifled a giggle and glanced across the room to where Derrick stood frozen, his jaw slightly open. Turning her gaze away from her Mr. Country Club ex, Maggie looked at Hunter. Derrick might be handsome, but the Ranger with the bedroom eyes was 100 percent sexier. "Tastes better with coffee. Great job, by the way. Nice and strong."

"You're welcome." He took another bite of the muffin.

"Maggie, we need to talk." Derrick's voice was strained, bordering on shrill.

"Whatever you need to say to Little Miss Maggie here, you can say in front of me," Hunter said.

Okay, maybe that was taking things a little too far. She wanted his presence to send Derrick packing for good, but Little Miss Maggie? No one who knew her would call her that. Derrick would see right through their little charade.

But then Hunter reached his free arm out, wrapped it around her waist and pulled her close, his hand spanning the curve between her rib cage and hip. Maggie nearly dropped her coffee mug. She knew it was a yeah-she's-mine-now move, but her body didn't care why he'd touched her again. Beneath her gray robe, she felt her nipples harden, remembering the way he'd teased her breasts last night on the porch.

Before she could protest or step away, he leaned down and nuzzled the back of her neck through her hair. He hit the spot that he knew would send her to heaven. He knew because she'd told him so on Saturday night. Memories of his mouth, his touch, the feel of him inside her, coursed through every nerve of her body, settling between her legs.

Maggie closed her eyes. Maybe it didn't matter what he called her. After witnessing this little scene, not even boring-in-bed Derrick would miss the fact that she'd been naked and intimate with her new friend.

Hunter's breath tickled the nape of her neck and a little moan escaped her lips. She wanted to throw off her clothes, wrap her body around him and tell Derrick to get the hell out of her kitchen unless he wanted to watch her come on the kitchen table.

Only she couldn't do that. Her scumbag ex stood five feet away and Hunter was her army liaison. She wasn't sure which one posed the bigger threat, but she suspected it was Hunter. Derrick had never sent her falling into head-over-heels-in-lust territory. He'd been the safe choice. Hunter should have a red danger sign across his chest.

Maggie stepped away, letting his arm fall from her waist. Instantly, she missed his touch. "Hunter, can you give us a minute?"

"Sure." He moved toward the screened porch, smiling at Derrick. "Thanks for bringing breakfast." He popped the rest of the muffin into his mouth as he stepped from the room.

"You're seeing someone?" Derrick asked, incredulous. "How long has this been going on?"

Like you have any right to ask. But she didn't want a fight about who cheated first. She knew the answer to that one. She wanted Derrick to leave and never come back.

"I can't believe you're seeing someone else," Derrick continued.

"Not exactly." Her head and body still spinning from Hunter's touch, Maggie struggled to find the words to explain her Saturday-night-fling-turned-liaison to the man she'd cast out of her life last week. "We met recently."

"Who is this guy? What do you know about him?" Derrick demanded, his hand cutting through the air to indicate the Ranger lounging on her porch.

"He's a friend, Derrick." She drained her coffee and went for a refill. "What are you doing here? I thought we were done."

"I want you back. I know I've made some mistakes."

Maggie snorted.

"I'm not always the best with romantic words," he continued as if he hadn't heard her. "But I know you, Maggie."

She looked at the stubborn expression on his face. Not pleading or begging, but pure determination.

"We're right for each other," he said. "I understand your career drive and your need to plan and organize everything. I understand you."

What about the me who wants mind-blowing sex? What about the me who wants more than stable and reliable? Looking at Derrick, she felt the smothering weight of all her responsibilities. A future with Derrick would not offer the relief she craved. The break she'd gone searching for Saturday night? It wasn't enough. The sex with Hunter had been a temporary fix. She realized that now. She possessed a wild side that was at odds with her need for control. Maggie wasn't sure how to resolve her inner turmoil, but she knew for a fact that lying, cheating Derrick was not the answer.

She downed another mouthful of coffee. "We belong together," Derrick continued.

"No, Derrick, we don't," she said flatly.

"That man out there," Derrick said, taking a step toward her. Maggie backed away. "He doesn't fit in your world, Maggie. He's not someone you take to a five-star restaurant, and you deserve five stars."

"No, I don't." Her hands tightened around her coffee mug as the anger she'd felt the day she'd found him with his pants down resurfaced. "I deserve a man who cares about me enough to remain faithful. I deserve a man who wants to be the responsible one—"

Derrick let out a mirthless laugh. "You would never let anyone else take charge, Maggie."

Maybe she didn't know how yet, but she could learn.

She'd let Hunter take control in bed, hadn't she? Of course, she'd panicked and run away while he slept. Still, it was a first step toward finding what she wanted.

"And orgasms," Maggie continued, pretending she hadn't heard Derrick's interruption. "I deserve orgasms. Nothing more, nothing less."

"Orgasms?" Derrick looked baffled as if her pleasure was a foreign concept. "What are you talking about?"

"I think you should go."

"But, Maggie, we're engaged. We've told everyone."

"Not anymore. We're done." The anger faded, leaving behind regret and irritation. But she wasn't only annoyed with Derrick. She was the one who had been a walk down the aisle away from marrying him, all because she thought she needed a man who would let her take charge of everything 24/7. And that wasn't Derrick's fault. That was on her.

She'd been too afraid of falling in love. Letting someone in was risky. It could turn her entire life upside down. But settling for common career interests and lousy sex? That was worse.

"I think you should take some time to think this over," Derrick said.

"No," she said firmly. "I gave the ring back to you and I told you we were through. I meant what I said. Now please leave, before I ask my friend out there to play bodyguard and show you out. And you can take the muffins."

RESTING HIS ELBOWS on his knees, Hunter leaned forward, watching Maggie and the Muffin Man. It didn't take a highly trained soldier to figure out that this wasn't a friendly thanks-for-breakfast conversation. Maggie looked stiff and tense. If she'd been a man with a weapon, he would have been worried. But he doubted she'd hurl her coffee mug at her early morning visitor, who looked more like a spoiled child who'd been told "no" than an adult.

Muffin Man? More like Muffin Boy.

Hunter smiled. A spoiled, rich boy was no match for him. While Muffin Boy had been perfecting his golf game, Hunter had completed the physically and mentally challenging Ranger School, hauling around ninety pounds of gear for twenty-plus hours a day. Not that he was competing for Maggie. He couldn't have her any more than Derrick could—especially after breaking into her computer last night. Actions like that didn't exactly inspire friendly feelings, never mind romantic ones.

Had her ex been after her heart? He watched Derrick through the glass windows. The man advanced toward Maggie. Hunter stood, ready to interrupt their private conversation, a rush of protectiveness pulsing through him. If Muffin Boy so much as laid a finger on Maggie, Hunter swore he'd tear the guy to pieces. But Maggie stepped away and Derrick stood still, taking the hint. Maggie wasn't about to let her ex invade her personal space.

Hunter sank back into his chair. She'd let him close. He was still hard from the feel of her body pressed against him. If they hadn't had an audience, he would have run his hand under her robe up to her breasts and kissed that special spot on her neck until she lost control of her senses. But if Derrick hadn't shown up on Maggie's doorstep, she'd never have let Hunter touch her. He'd known the minute she'd picked up the muffin that she was using him to scare off her visitor.

The thought of being used—first for orgasms, then for her book and now to scare away the man she'd been trying to forget Saturday night—should have discouraged his erection like a jump into ice-cold water, but it didn't. Hunter shifted in his chair, silently cursing himself for not wearing something other than jeans. It seemed the lower half of his body wanted her and didn't care about why she'd let him wrap his arm around her and pull her close.

Being used? Yeah, it should have pissed him off. But Maggie was a means to an end for him, also. He wasn't here to win her heart or a place in her bed—though he certainly wouldn't turn down a trip to her bedroom.

Hunter watched Maggie set down her coffee, pick up the muffin box and shove it into Derrick's chest. That was his cue, he decided, heading for the door to the kitchen. They'd had time to talk. Now it was time for Muffin Boy to walk out the front door. Hunter fully intended to help him find his way if he didn't head for the exit in five, four, three, two—

Derrick set the box on the counter and turned to the swinging door just as Hunter stepped into the room.

"I mean it, Derrick," Maggie said. "No more phone calls, no more harassing my friends at work. Nothing. This is the end."

"Goodbye, Maggie," Derrick said, one hand on the door. He glanced over at Hunter. "I hope you know what you're doing."

The door swung closed behind Derrick, and Hunter turned to Maggie.

"I'm sorry about that," she said, slumping into a chair at the kitchen counter. "I probably should have told you my ex might show up."

"And ruin the surprise? I only met the guy for a few minutes, but he didn't seem like your type."

"He said the same thing about you."

Hunter saw a soft smile on her lips. Pleased she didn't look crestfallen over Derrick anymore, he went over to her fridge and opened it up.

"He's probably right," he said, rummaging through the

meager contents of the shelves. The startling need he'd felt to jump in and rescue her from her ex had left him unsettled. Why should he be concerned about her relationship with her former fiancé? She wasn't his family.

But the whys didn't matter. The fact was he cared, and he needed to make damn certain she took the necessary steps to protect herself. "Have you thought about taking out a restraining order against your early morning visitor?"

"For Derrick? I don't think that's necessary. He won't be back."

Hunter pulled out a half-full carton of eggs and checked the date. "Rejection can make a man do stupid things, especially if he thinks the woman he loves has moved on to someone else."

"Derrick doesn't love me."

"He wanted to marry you," Hunter said, surprised by the certainty in her voice. "And correct me if I'm wrong here, but you said yes."

Maggie shook her head. "We have similar interests. He's a political science professor with a focus on peace treaties."

Hunter raised an eyebrow.

"It's more interesting than it sounds," she said.

"That's your criteria for marriage? If I was going to commit to 'until death do us part,' I'd want more than similar interests."

He set the eggs on the counter.

Maggie sighed. "I thought what was between us would be enough. But now I realize I need more. I need…"

Hunter sensed she was struggling to find the right words.

"I need to trust the man I marry," she continued.

"You didn't trust Muffin Boy?"

Maggie laughed, but didn't smile. "I did until I caught him with one of his research assistants."

He'd cheated on her. Maggie wasn't someone who trusted easily and the bastard had taken that trust and destroyed it. Part of him wished Muffin Boy had given him an excuse to land a punch on his pretty-boy face. Hell, if Muffin Boy showed up again, he'd strip down to his boxers before answering the door. Let the bastard think he'd just come from Maggie's bed.

But he wouldn't be staying in her guest bedroom forever. If he had his way, he'd be out of there in a week, maybe less, and back on active duty, leading his team. Who knew how and when Derrick might strike again.

"A broken heart can make a man do stupid things," he said. "Christ, Maggie, he showed up at your doorstep with a box of muffins."

"I sent him away. It's over."

"For now. If he comes back with something more threatening than muffins and I'm not here, you bolt the door and call the cops, okay?"

She nodded. That was the best he could do for now.

"How about I whip us up some eggs and toast?" he asked, opening the egg carton. "That tasteless, fat-free thing didn't do it for me."

"You can cook?"

"You don't need to sound so surprised. Breakfast is my specialty." Turning around, he opened a cabinet and found a glass bowl. Returning to the island, he cracked two eggs into the bowl and began whipping them with a fork. "I'm hoping if I impress you with my cooking skills you might let me crash in your guest room again. It's a hell of a lot nicer than the motel."

She hesitated. "I don't think that's a good idea. We need to maintain a professional relationship."

He set down the bowl and studied her. Those loose blond curls, that smooth skin and those bright blue eyes—

he wanted her more than he'd wanted anything in a long time. Looking at her now, he realized that the reasons he couldn't have her paled in comparison to his desire.

He turned his gaze to the open fields beyond her. He'd ridden a freaking horse through Afghanistan on a saddle made out of wooden boards and goat hide. He'd negotiated with warlords, evaded capture more times than he wanted to count and completed dozens of successful recon missions. He was a goddamn U.S. army ranger. He could keep his personal and work life separate. The question was could she?

"What happens if we don't?" he asked.

"If anyone found out, your colonel, my editor," Maggie said. "It's not professional. I can't sleep with you and interview you."

"Not at the same time." Hunter went to her side, put his hands on her waist and turned her to look at him. He kept his hold on her, feeling her body tense with nerves and indecision. "But what if we kept the two separate? We'll do the interviews during the day, and then at night…"

He leaned forward and brushed his lips against her ear. "At night, you're mine."

"Yours?" She lifted her hands to his chest, but she didn't push him away.

"Whatever drew us together that first night—lust, chemistry, call it whatever you want. It's still here between us. You feel it, too, don't you?"

"Yes," she whispered.

"I made a promise to you that first night, Maggie. A promise to blow your fantasies out of the water." He drew back. "Look at me, Maggie." She lifted her gaze to meet his and he saw the desire in her eyes.

"But that was just for one night—"

"I'm not asking you for a commitment, Maggie. I don't

do long term. I'm here for as long as this assignment lasts, but that's it. I'm not going to lie to you. You have my word on that. I'm not your ex. But none of that changes the fact I made a promise to you, and I keep my promises."

11

ONE MINUTE HE'D been making eggs, the picture of domesticity, and the next he had her body purring with need, asking her to throw away her career for wild leave-your-control-at-the-door sex.

Deep down Maggie knew the career risk was an excuse. Yes, having sex with an interview subject was unprofessional, but once she finished interviewing Hunter, the lines blurred. Even then, fear would linger, holding her back. If she went to bed with him again, he'd claim control of her body, bringing her sexual fantasies to life. Part of her wanted that. Desperately. But she wasn't sure she was ready. If the panic she'd felt Saturday night had taught her anything, it was that letting a man take charge involved trust. And she wasn't sure she could trust the injured Ranger standing in front of her.

Hunter cupped her jaw with his hand, his thumb stroking her cheek, forcing her to meet his gaze. "Say yes, Maggie."

"I'll think about it." It was the best she could do.

Smiling, he released her and went back to cooking. "Don't think too long. I'm not here forever."

No, he wasn't. This might be her only chance to make

her fantasies come true. She clenched her thighs. Work. She had to work before they could play. "But first I want an interview. A real one."

"Okay." He opened a cabinet. "Where are your plates?"

"Above the dishwasher." She hesitated. She had to know, before this thing between them went any further, didn't she? "There's something else."

"Shoot."

Who's Sierra? The words were on the tip of her tongue, but she remained silent. He was offering her a chance to be a wild, sexy woman at night and to focus on her work during the day. Part of her wanted to push away her reservations and say yes. Part of her wanted to pretend she'd never overheard his conversation. Could she do that? Bury her head in the sand for a few days? Sierra could be a cousin or family friend.

Or she could be his girlfriend, and mentioning her name would end the fantasy before it had even begun.

"Maggie?" he prompted.

"It's nothing." When they'd first met, he'd told her and Olivia that he was unmarried. She would have to take him at his word. If going to bed with him meant trusting him, it had to start here and now. "Just that I like my eggs cooked through."

SEVEN HOURS LATER, Maggie collapsed onto a kitchen chair, exhausted. She'd conducted dozens of interviews, but none like this one. He'd answered all of her prepared questions except the one she was burning to ask.

How do you plan to blow my fantasies out of the water?

She had a feeling he knew that question stood front and center in her mind. His gaze fell to her lips when she spoke, drifting farther south on more than one occasion. Not that she'd behaved much better. She'd spent the entire interview undressing him with her eyes, which had left parts of her aching and wanting. Very professional.

When she'd suggested they break for a few hours, he'd agreed. She'd offered him lunch, but he'd turned down food in favor of a run. She'd spent an hour working on her blog before she'd set out for a run, too. Then straight to the fridge for leftover pasta, grabbing the phone on her way. After this morning, she didn't trust herself to make this decision—to sleep with him or not—on her own. She needed another opinion.

"Olivia?" Maggie pressed her cell phone between her ear and shoulder as she rummaged through the fridge. "I need to get out tonight."

"Ready for another one-night stand already? What about your Ranger?"

Maggie pulled a half-eaten container of pasta from the bottom shelf and set it on the counter. "He refuses to stay at his motel. He insists my guest room is more comfortable."

"The downstairs one with the fancy marble shower?" Olivia asked. "No one in their right mind would stay at a motel when they could have access to that shower."

"Well, that doesn't change the fact that he is still here and that I need a break." She opened the silverware drawer and selected a fork. "A girls' night out."

"Did you have someplace in mind?" Olivia asked.

"Frida's. I want guacamole and margaritas." She'd been on the bride-to-be, low-fat-muffin diet for too long. If she was going to let herself go, she might as well go all the way.

"It's ladies' night at Frida's. It will be packed with single men," Olivia warned.

"And single women. The men won't even look at me. I'll wear my usual boring clothes. Something gray. I promise."

"And a bra?"

"Yes, I promise to wear a bra." The kitchen door swung

open as the words crossed her lips and a shirtless, sweaty U.S. army ranger sauntered into the room. Her mouth went dry and her fork fell into the take-out container. Setting the pasta on the counter, she reached for her water and took a gulp.

"I've got to go," she said once she'd swallowed. "I'll meet you there at seven."

Maggie studied the rim of her glass, determined not to stare at the way his waist narrowed until it disappeared from view, hidden by his running shorts. If she looked, she'd want to touch, and she couldn't touch. Not yet. "I'm going out with Olivia. A girls' night out."

"And this time you're wearing a bra," he said, his voice a low rumble.

"Exactly." She picked up the cell phone without looking at him. She could feel his eyes on her chest as if he was trying to determine if she was wearing one now. Her traitorous breasts responded to the heated look and the building tension between them.

"You're on your own for dinner," she said quickly, moving toward the door. "But there should be plenty of left-overs in the fridge. Help yourself. And you're free for the rest of the afternoon. I have some work I need to finish on my computer."

"Maggie." His hand wrapped around her arm, gently pulling her to a stop. Every nerve ending in her body jumped to attention, both annoying and thrilling her at the same time. What was it about this man that turned her on so much? She met his heated gaze. No question he felt it, too, and God if that didn't turn her on more. "Don't think too long."

She nodded as he released her arm, not trusting herself to speak in case the only words that came out of her mouth were "Orgasm. Now." And then she hustled into the hall.

BY SEVEN-THIRTY Maggie and Olivia were seated in a corner booth at Frida's. Maggie dug a chip into the mammoth bowl of guacamole on the table. One margarita down and she already felt better. She chased her chip with a sip from her second frozen taste of heaven. When was the last time she'd said, "Screw the low-calorie beer, I'm having tequila"? So long ago, she couldn't remember. She couldn't even recall the last time she'd been to Frida's. Probably before Derrick, and even then she'd never braved ladies' night.

But tonight she didn't care. She'd worn jeans, canvas slip-ons and her old gray hooded sweatshirt over a white tank top. Her underwear, including her bra, was boring beige. No one, man or woman, spared her a second glance, and she didn't bother looking at them. She kept her eyes on the guacamole and her drink.

"How's everything with the Ranger?" Olivia asked over the rim of her sangria.

Maggie looked up. Olivia had decided to dress for ladies' night. A man would have to be blind to miss her friend's bright orange blouse and white pencil skirt. "He's driving me crazy."

"You could ask him to leave."

"I don't want him to leave. I don't have a book without him. That's part of the problem."

"And the other part?"

"I want to tear my clothes off every time I see him."

"Not very professional." Olivia caught their server's attention and signaled for another round.

"He's the one who started it. If he'd just stay at his motel."

"To be fair, you started it. You're the one who picked him up at the car show," Olivia pointed out.

"I started a one-night stand. He's trying to make it

into something more." Maggie set aside her empty second drink. Just saying those words made her body tingle with need. Or maybe that was the alcohol. She was starting to feel a little fuzzy. "I just keep wondering, what would happen if I let him?"

"Let him what?"

"Touch me. See me naked. Again," Maggie said as the server deposited their drinks and scurried away into the crowd of women.

"You would have sex." Olivia spoke loud enough for the table next to theirs to pause mid-conversation to listen.

"Liv, that's part of the problem." Maggie leaned forward, dropping her voice to a near whisper. "This isn't just sex. He made me a promise."

Olivia leaned in. "What sort of promise? And why are we whispering?"

"We're in public." She looked down at her drink. "And this is personal."

"Go on."

Maggie hesitated. But this was what best friends were for—spilling secrets over margaritas and asking for drunken advice. "He promised it would be better than my wildest dreams."

"And this is a problem because?"

"I've never told you this." Maggie met her friend's questioning gaze. "I've never told anyone this. Except Hunter. But he didn't count at the time because I never thought I'd see him again." She paused and took a breath. "I have some pretty wild fantasies."

"Good for you." Olivia reached out and patted her hand. "You're wound up so tight from all the pressure you put on yourself that sometimes I worry you might explode. Like I told you Saturday, sex is just what you need. Look at it this way, you're simply searching for a way to vent your sexual frustration and explore your hidden desires so that you can concentrate on your work."

When Olivia put it like that, it sounded completely sane. Why shouldn't she have sex with Hunter? She wasn't looking for a ring and a promise from him. As long as she knew that up front, what did she have to worry about? Olivia might be right, if she wanted to focus on her work, put her book first, she *should* sleep with him. She turned this logic over in her tequila-filled mind. "Maybe you're right."

"Of course I'm right. He offered to fulfill your fantasies, for goodness' sake. Go get him!"

"I need to call a cab." Maggie pushed back from the table and pulled her wallet out of her purse. Tossing a pair of twenties on the table, she looked at Olivia. "Will you be okay if I leave?"

"Go." Olivia made a shooing motion with her hands. "Have sex. And don't forget to come back for your car in the morning."

Five minutes later, Maggie slid into a cab and gave the driver her address. Before she reached for her seat belt, she pulled her arms into her sweatshirt.

"Hey, lady, what are you doing back there?" the driver called.

Maggie met his gaze in the rearview mirror. "Losing my bra. Just keep your eyes on the road."

12

MAGGIE MIGHT HAVE finished her work for the day but his wasn't complete. She'd hidden in her office all afternoon, and Hunter had a hunch she'd been working on her blog. He had to know what she'd written before he could wonder about her answer to his other question.

With his hand on the door to her study, he was on the verge of saying, *To hell with it all, just get her naked and into bed.* Promising her interviews with every Ranger he'd ever worked with. The moon. Anything.

But if he failed this mission, he wouldn't be the only one to suffer. He could lose the job he loved and the money he needed to support Sierra. One more overdose and he could lose his sister forever. She deserved a fresh start, and he'd make damn sure she got it.

He opened the door to Maggie's study. He'd heard the Mercedes peel out of the driveway fifteen minutes ago. Now was his chance. But when he sat down in front of her computer, he hesitated.

If he changed her blog, deleting any information about his injury and any reference to his team as a bunch of cow-boys, there was no going back. Once she found out, Maggie would hate him. He'd be cast out of her life as quickly as Muffin Boy.

His hands rested on top of her laptop but didn't move. That first night at the Marriott, she'd handed him her trust when she'd let him call the shots, and now he felt the weight of it. It was like carrying a forty-pound sack rigged with C4 into a mission. And Miss Maggie's feelings didn't end there. He was pretty damn sure she desired him almost as much as he did her. He saw the way she looked at him when he entered the house without his shirt. Her eyes exclaimed *green light, come and get me,* while her body stepped away.

If she lost faith in him, she'd never welcome him into her bed again. He'd had enough dancing around the hot connection between them. He'd rather ride another wild horse through Taliban country than sit through a second full day of questions with a hard-on. But to give her what she wanted, to coax the wild pound-the-bed-as-she-shatters Maggie out of her shell, she had to trust him.

Making a woman's sexual fantasies come true had never been high on his to-do list. He generally preferred his sex hard and fast. With Maggie, the idea of taking away her control, having her completely dependent on him for her pleasure, really did it for him. And it didn't stop there. He liked her.

His hands fell away from the closed computer and landed on his lap.

He admired her courage. She went after what she wanted, pushing her nerves aside like a soldier on a mission. It didn't matter if her goal was an orgasm or her book, she went for it. Her determination to look beyond her own lousy childhood with a drunken ex-Ranger for a father and see the good side of what soldiers did every day damn near floored him.

Hunter pushed back from the desk. He couldn't do it Hell, it wasn't as if the colonel had specifically ordered him to take down her blog. For all he knew, she'd already changed the content based on their interviews. He'd never know if he didn't ask her first. And maybe, if he talked to her, she'd agree to make some changes. Maggie wasn't the enemy here. And this wasn't a run-of-the-mill recon mission. Maybe this time subterfuge wasn't the only way

In his pocket, his phone vibrated. Hunter pulled it out, immediately recognizing the Tennessee area code. He pressed a button and answered. "Cross."

"Chief," his colonel said. "How are things in New York? Keeping a tight leash on the professor?"

"Yes, sir." Hunter leaned back in Maggie's desk chair and looked out the window across the fields. "Though so far I don't think we have much to worry about. I don't think Professor Barlow is digging for secrets."

"Good," his commanding officer replied. "But we need confirmation that book of hers won't raise any questions. Get a look at her notes and whatever else she's written Read it, and if it's all clear, we'll talk about bringing you home to run your team after the interviews."

His team. Hell, if he didn't love the sound of that. "Yes, sir," he said. "Will do."

Hunter slipped his phone back into his pocket and looked at the computer. The lieutenant hadn't said a word about her blog. He wasn't disobeying his orders by leaving it alone. But her manuscript was another story.

He had a USB drive in his pocket and her password. He could download her notes and latest draft, read it tonight and be home running his team early next week after the other interviews were complete.

And hope she never found out he'd gone behind her back.

Hunter pushed back from the desk, leaving her computer untouched. He'd find another way to gain access—one that didn't violate her trust.

He glanced at the study door. How safe she felt with him didn't matter much if she didn't come home before dawn. The image of Maggie dressed up in her Saturday-night clothes, approaching another man and uttering those words...

I want an amazing orgasm. Actually, scratch that. I want more than one.

No, he'd caught a glimpse of her before she'd driven away to meet Olivia. Gray sweatshirt, old jeans and sneakers—she hadn't looked like a woman hunting for a one-night stand. But a few days under Little Miss Maggie's spell and Hunter knew she could have men falling at her feet with one look from those blue eyes. A gray sweatshirt couldn't hide the full curve of her breasts. She could wear a grain sack and a man would still want to reach out and touch.

Click.

He snapped to attention. Someone had just walked into the house. Quickly and silently, he stood and made his way to the study door. He pressed his ear to the wood. In the hall, he heard footsteps followed by the sound of the kitchen door swinging open.

"Hunter?" Maggie called.

He glanced at the digital clock on her desk. Nine o'clock. She'd come home early. He had to get out of here. His training kicked in, and without making a sound, he slipped into the hall just as he would an enemy camp.

When Maggie pushed through the swinging door, barreling into him, Hunter felt a pang of guilt for what he'd done. He hadn't touched her computer. This time. Still, he shouldn't have been there in the first place. But the feel of Maggie in his arms went straight to his groin and the guilt faded into the background. Her chest pressed against him. He raised his hands to her arms, half expecting her to jump away from him if he didn't grab onto her. She didn't move. She just stood there, looking up at him, her eyes wide. Her tongue darted out of her mouth and slid over her pink lips.

Nope, that definitely wasn't guilt he was feeling now. It was pure lust.

His gaze slid down from her mouth to the insanely large purse hanging from her shoulder. Did she have condoms in there? He didn't see a box peeking out. But—

Beige bra strap. He blinked, his eyes narrowing as he studied the indisputable evidence that Little Miss Maggie had abandoned her underwear.

Jealousy, the kind usually reserved for people in committed relationships, pounded through his veins. He released his hold on her. She wasn't his. He had no right to feel possessive of her. None. But hell, he wanted to hit something. It killed him not knowing why she'd taken off her bra.

He looked to her feet. No flip-flops. Maybe she hadn't taken the time to remove her shoes. The image of Maggie pressed up against the wall of a dirty bar flew through his mind. His hands fisted at his sides. She might not be his, but he still wanted to pound the living hell out of anyone who'd dared to touch her.

"There you are." She offered him a shy, yet sultry smile. This was his Saturday-night Maggie. Except her breath smelled heavily of tequila.

Hunter unclenched his jaw. "Have fun?"

"Not yet."

What the—

The need to hit something faded and his brain kicked into gear. Maggie was here. Braless. And ready for fun. Gold star for the Ranger, who'd used his *think first, act second* training to put two and two together. Miss Maggie had stripped off her underwear for him. Too bad she'd chosen tonight, right after he'd fought a moral battle over whether or not to break into her computer.

Hunter took a step back, the realization hitting him hard like a punch to the gut. He couldn't do this. Not here in the hall. Not tonight.

This wasn't just another fling. He cared about Maggie. He couldn't afford a committed relationship, but she deserved better than a man who'd spent the evening debating whether to invade her privacy. She ought to be wined and dined. She deserved honesty. And for what he had in mind for her, she deserved a bed.

Maggie stepped closer. Too close. He moved away, backing into the wall.

"Where are you going?" she asked.

"Maggie, you've been drinking and we shouldn't do this. Not tonight." He needed to talk to her first, when she was sober. He had to find a way to follow his orders, get his promotion and keep his sister in rehab without going behind Maggie's back.

"Shh." She pressed her right index finger against his lips. His mouth begged to lick and kiss it. She ran her left hand up his neck into his hair. One step closer and—

Oh, hell.

Maggie pinned him to the wall, her chest pressed up against his. Unable to stop himself, he glanced down. Inside her gray sweatshirt, he could see the tops of her round braless breasts rising above her white tank top. His jeans went from tight to unbearable. Hunter closed his eyes and groaned.

"Hunter?"

He felt the word against his lips as she drew his head down, her fingers firmly laced in his hair. God help him, he let her. He prided himself on his mental ability to endure. Hell, he'd been trained to go without food and sleep while on missions. But go without Maggie now?

Her lips touched his. Gently. Not a real kiss. Not yet. He could still step away. But then her tongue licked across his closed mouth, asking, then demanding entrance, and desire squashed his self-control like a bug.

He kissed her back, opening his mouth against hers. His arms wrapped around her, drawing her closer to him, trapping her against him. His erection pressed against her stomach, threatening to explode just from the tequila-filled taste of her.

She'd come home to him. The first woman in as long as he could remember whom he wanted to wake up next to in the morning had run home to him.

And nearly caught him sitting at her desk, his hands on her computer.

His fingers froze on her back and his lips stopped moving. Ignoring the throbbing in his groin, he grasped for her waist and gently pushed her away.

"Hunter?"

"We can't do this," he repeated.

She pressed her palms against his chest. "Why not? No one has to know. Not your colonel, not my editor. We're just two people venting a little sexual frustration."

Her devilish hands ran up over his collarbone to his shoulders. Her fingers kneaded his tense muscles, a powerful reminder of everything she'd offered him in his hotel room.

"I know you want me. You said so yourself." He heard her voice over the roaring pleasure coursing through his body.

"I do, Maggie. But not like this. You're drunk," he managed to say. If he had any hope of getting away, he had to leave now. He was a man. He could only resist so much.

"Maybe a little," she said.

He had to step away. Hunter closed his eyes. Maybe if he didn't look at the soft curls falling from her bun, or her intent blue eyes. Maybe if he didn't steal another glance down her sweatshirt, he could escape. His honor demanded it. He could not have the kind of hold-nothing-back wild ride they both craved until he deserved her trust.

Mentally preparing to make his move, he tightened his grip on her waist, willing his arms to set her aside. But as his fingers pressed into her clothes, her hands fell away from his shoulders and she stepped back.

His eyes flew open.

"I want you." She stepped out of her shoes and kicked them aside. "Now."

Those four little words nearly undid his resolve. She pulled her sweatshirt up over her head. Her pebbled nipples strained at the thin white tank top.

"I want you," she repeated. "Fast and hard."

Her tank top followed her sweatshirt to the ground and he was a goner. Little Miss Maggie had won. Knowing he'd probably hate himself in the morning, he reached out and touched her breast.

MAGGIE MOANED, LEANING into his touch. She'd won. He'd given in to the powerful attraction between them. It probably helped that she'd removed her shirt.

Hunter's fingers traced small circles around her nipples, sending ripples of bliss through her body. She'd go crazy if she didn't kiss him soon. Maggie drew his mouth down to hers, but his free hand captured her arm, gently returning it to her side.

"No," he said. "Let me take control. That's what you want, isn't it?"

"Yes," she gasped. She heard the hard edge in his voice, but ignored it. This—his fingers teasing her breast—felt too heavenly to think about anything else but the sensations on her skin and the ache building between her thighs. "Oh, God, yes."

She heard him grunt as he pushed her jeans over her hips one-handed. His other hand teased her to the point where she wondered if she might have an orgasm before he removed her underwear.

"Close your eyes," he demanded.

She obeyed.

His hand gave one final push and her old, worn jeans slid down her legs to her ankles, exposing her plain beige and very damp bikini briefs. Damp? Make that soaked. Knowing he was looking at her while she stood nearly naked in front of him with her eyes closed turned her on more than she could have imagined.

"Spread your legs."

Her brow furrowed. With her jeans around her ankles, she could barely move. "How?"

"As far as you can."

Maggie stepped as wide as her jeans would allow. As if rewarding her for following his orders, he ran his hand down her belly, gliding his fingers under the elastic band of her underwear, and she understood. He'd positioned her just wide enough to explore and touch her, but if she tried to move away, she'd become tangled in her jeans and fall. She was trapped, his to do with as he pleased.

She gasped. The thought of being completely under his control sent spasms rushing through her body. She'd never been this turned on. Ever. Yet she wasn't afraid.

She trusted him to give her what she needed, to fulfill her fantasy.

His fingers ran back and forth over her most sensitive part, not teasing, but driving her toward completion. She was close. So close. On the verge of an Orgasm—capital *O*. His breath teased her neck and the muscles between her legs clenched. Keeping one hand between her legs and the other on her breast, he gently suckled the side of her neck.

It was too much. She couldn't hold back any longer. Pleasure radiated from her core until her knees went weak. She leaned into him for support as if she were a rag doll. Her head rested on his shoulder as the most powerful orgasm she'd ever experienced ebbed and flowed, refusing to fade away altogether.

When she finally returned to herself—granted, a much happier, sated version—and caught her breath, Maggie reached between them. She ran her hand over his T-shirt until she found the top of his jeans. She tugged at the button until it released, then moved to his zipper. Her fingers brushed his erection through his boxers and she heard him groan. Even through his shorts, he felt hot, hard and ready. She didn't care if he kept his clothes on and pinned her to the wall. She just wanted him inside her.

"One down. Are you ready for another?" she asked, echoing his words from last Saturday night.

He gently released her breast and took hold of her wrist. Carefully, he set her hand away from him. She opened her eyes, lifted her head and looked at him. Did he plan to take charge? No, his tight-lipped expression was far too serious for a man about to have wild sex in a hallway.

"No, Maggie," he said. "We shouldn't. Not like this."

"Why not?" Emboldened by the intoxicating mix of alcohol and orgasm, she slipped her hand beneath the elastic waistband of his boxers until her fingers brushed against the tip of his erection.

"You deserve more," he said without conviction.

"I want this." She wrapped her hand around him.

"Tomorrow night, Maggie." His voice was low and rough. "Tomorrow I'm going to make you lose control. But not now. Not here in the hall after you've downed half a bottle of tequila."

Her body still basking in the afterglow of the amazing orgasm he'd given her, Maggie watched as he zipped up his pants and walked away. She waited for the oh-God-what-have-I-done feeling to wash over her. After all, she'd let him take control of her body and asked for more. But instead, anticipation flooded her from head to toe. Tomorrow night he was going to make her sexual fantasies come true. And she trusted him to deliver on that promise.

HUNTER STOMPED INTO his room and headed for the shower. Stripping off his shoes, followed by his clothes, he stepped under the blasting water. He could still feel the full weight of Maggie's breast in his hand. The taste of her skin lingered on his tongue and lips. Her cries as she came echoed in his mind.

It had taken every ounce of self-control and then some to walk away from her. But she deserved better than a quick, drunken encounter in a hall. That didn't change the fact he'd rather endure a fifteen-mile march in full gear through a hailstorm than force himself to leave a naked Maggie again. If she came looking for him right now, there was no chance in hell he would send her away. He'd probably pull her into the shower, press her up against the wall and push his way inside of her.

Groaning, he let his mind run wild with images of Maggie wet and naked, whispering the same words she'd said earlier. *I want you. Fast and hard.*

He needed release. His body begged for it and he wouldn't be able to think clearly until he took the edge off the sexual energy pulsing through him. Wrapping his right hand around himself, he moved up and down his erection. His mind went straight to Maggie, picturing her naked breasts, the curve of her waist, the curls between her legs.

He increased the pressure, pumping his hand faster and faster. Earlier, in the hall, she had been wet and ready for him, her body eagerly accepting his fingers inside her, her muscles tightening around him. He remembered the way her face had tensed and then relaxed as she'd come hard against his hand, and his body responded, letting go of everything he'd been resisting. Hunter cried out, tossing his head back as he came, allowing the water to run over his face.

Once he'd caught his breath, he reached for the soap and began to clean himself up. He'd taken care of his immediate need, but that didn't change the fact that he wanted Maggie. She'd sought him out to fulfill her fantasies and now he wanted to explore some of his own. Nothing too wild or rough, but he still required her faith that he'd never hurt her. Standing under the powerful spray of warm water, he knew exactly what he had to do.

13

Knock, knock.

Reaching one hand out from beneath her covers, Maggie felt around on the nightstand for her alarm clock and hit it over and over. The knocking continued. If this was all in her head, it was hands down the worst hangover of her life.

"Wake up, honey," a male voice called from the hallway. "You have an interview in an hour."

Slowly, she sat up, blinking at the light pouring in through the windows. She'd forgotten to close the curtains before she'd fallen into bed last night, drunk from too much tequila. Or maybe she'd just been in a daze from the best orgasm of her life provided by the man who refused to have sex with her.

Until tonight. Maggie smiled.

"Maggie?" Hunter called again. "I said the magic word. You have an *interview*."

"I'm coming." She moved as quickly as her still-sluggish limbs would allow, shrugging on her robe. The smell of fresh-brewed French roast hit her as soon as she opened the door and her gaze focused on the mug in his hands. "Coffee?"

"I figured you might need a cup after last night."

"I always need coffee in the morning." Grateful, she took the mug and brought it to her lips. He'd added just the right amount of cream. "It's perfect." Maggie looked up at his smiling face. "Did you say something about interviews?"

"I took the liberty of setting up an interview with Riley."

"Your teammate who lives around here?"

"Yes, but he has family visiting so he asked if you could Skype at nine this morning before his mother-in-law arrives."

"Sure, Skype works." She preferred to meet in person, but decided she'd ask for a face-to-face follow-up if she needed to speak with Riley again.

"I also set up the interviews with the guys at the base for Saturday morning."

Maggie felt the sides of her mouth dip into a frown. "You've been busy."

Hunter shrugged. "I couldn't sleep much last night. But I still need to book the flights."

"I'll take care of that." Common sense told her Hunter was simply doing his job as her liaison, but it felt an awful lot like he wanted to take charge. She'd given him control of her orgasms, not her work.

"If you think you'll have time," Hunter said.

"I was planning to use the morning to write a rough chapter or two based on yesterday's interview. I'll start on that after I talk to your friend. But I think I can spare the time to book plane tickets."

Hunter nodded. "Sounds good. I'd like to read what you have so far." He reached out and tucked a strand of hair behind her ear. The simple touch left her skin tingling. "If you're willing to share, of course. I thought it might help if I checked to make sure the details are all there. See if you're missing any key parts before you meet the rest of the guys."

"Sure, that would be great. I can print the pages for you before lunch. While you're doing that—"

"You can go on a little shopping trip," he interrupted.

Maggie frowned. "Are we out of something? The housekeeper comes today. I could have her pick up anything you need."

"Unless she's in the habit of buying your shoes, I think this is one errand you're going to need to run yourself."

"My shoes?" Even with the jolt from the coffee, he wasn't making sense. "What's wrong with my shoes?"

"They're too low." Hunter's fingers brushed her cheek, and this time he didn't pull back after adjusting her fresh-out-of-bed hair. He cradled her jaw in the palm of his hand. Her pulse raced. He closed the space between them until his chest brushed up against her hands. The only thing between them was her coffee cup. He leaned forward, his lips so close to her left ear she could feel his breath.

"Tonight's my turn, Maggie," he said, his voice low and sensual. "And my fantasies? They involve high heels. The highest you can find."

"Your fantasies?" she squeaked, her eyes widening. This was not the conversation she'd imagined having over morning coffee.

"Don't worry, Miss Maggie. You can trust me. I won't hurt you. What I have in mind isn't rough." He drew back and met her gaze. "Just a little sweet."

"Sweet," she repeated. Lust fought her hangover and won. Her nipples hardened, desperate to know what he had planned for her.

"Just buy the shoes, Maggie."

She nodded. There was no way she'd refuse him, especially not after last night. She wanted to feel that way again. Out of control with passion, but without the oh-God-what-have-I-done panic.

He stepped back and she felt the loss of his touch. "I'm going for a run before it gets too hot out there. The info you need to contact Riley is on the kitchen counter."

Maggie nodded again. She watched him disappear down the stairs and then made a beeline for the phone.

"Morning," Olivia said when she answered. "I thought you'd still be in bed."

"I need to go shoe shopping," she blurted. "Today. This afternoon."

"I never thought I'd hear you say those words. I'll meet you at the mall on my lunch hour. Noon by the entrance to Macy's."

MAGGIE FOUND OLIVIA standing at the door to the mall with two large cups of coffee. She thrust one at Maggie. "You'll need this. We have to move quickly. I have to be back at the gallery in two hours. First, we're going to Macy's, then Nordstrom's."

She took the coffee. "I only need one pair of shoes, Liv."

Olivia led the way past the makeup counters, through the handbags to ladies' shoes. "What kind of shoes are we talking about here?"

"High heels. Really high."

Her friend stopped in front of the sandals display. "You can barely manage two inches, Maggs."

A blush crept up Maggie's cheeks. "I don't think I'll be doing much walking in these."

Olivia smiled. "I take it last night was a success?"

"No. I mean, yes, but not entirely." Maggie closed her eyes and refocused her thoughts. "I don't know what I'm doing with him. He's wrong for me. I mean, an injured

Ranger? But I can't help it, Liv, I want one more night in his bed."

"There's a reason they call it crazy in love," Olivia said in a singsong voice.

Maggie frowned. "This isn't love. It's lust."

Olivia raised an eyebrow. "You don't have feelings for him?"

"I respect him. He's a hero. The real deal. And he's fun." She remembered the meal they'd shared that first night in his hotel room. "He's good company. But that's it."

"If you're sure."

"He's only in this for the short term, Liv. He's been very clear."

"As long as you're both on the same page. I'd hate to see you get hurt, especially so soon after Derrick."

"He promised he wouldn't hurt me." *In bed.* "And I trust him."

Olivia grabbed her hand. "Great. Let's find you the perfect pair of heels."

Ten pairs of shoes later, Maggie finally put the salesman out of his misery and bought a pair of sheer black lace, peep-toe Jimmy Choo pumps with a ridiculous five-inch heel. She doubted she'd ever wear them again. She even questioned whether she could stand, never mind walk in them.

"Maggs, there's a man waving at us." Olivia pointed across the shoe department. "Pink button-down. The one who looks like he could be Derrick's twin."

Maggie slipped her feet back into her boring but oh-so-comfortable flats and saw her colleague Professor Dan Eglebrauch walking toward them. She'd never noticed the similarities before, but the man did look a lot like her ex.

"Professor Barlow, good to see you," he said with too

much enthusiasm for a man she rarely saw outside of faculty meetings.

"Hello, Dan." She stood, grateful he hadn't caught her trying on skyscraper heels. It was bad enough that he'd report back to all his cronies, her fellow professors, that he'd run into her shoe shopping when her book was due in a matter of months.

"I heard about your book deal," he said. "The whole department is talking about it. Sounds like I'll be teaching some of your classes when school starts up again so you can take the semester off to finish it. How's the research going? Getting close to having a first draft?"

"The book is coming along. I interviewed the Ranger who led the team this morning."

"Exciting stuff."

Maggie nodded. Riley had basically repeated the same information she'd learned from Hunter. When she'd asked how Hunter had been shot, he'd fed her the same line Hunter had—classified. She'd pressed him for details, but he'd stonewalled her.

"I'm taking a quick break and then it's back to writing."

"If you can spare the time, I'm hosting an informal pool party tonight before Carter takes off for his summer vacation. His wife's dragging him on a cruise this year."

Informal pool party translated to schmoozing their colleagues on the tenure review board. And while the other members were important, Carter led the committee. Whoever he championed for tenure would win.

The drive to succeed that had propelled Maggie through school after her father's life fell apart flared up. If Carter voted for her, she'd have tenure. No one could take that away from her.

"Just a few of the guys from the political science department and their wives," Dan continued. "Would you like to join us?"

"Yes, I'd—"

"She can't," Olivia interrupted. "Her army liaison is in town and she's meeting him tonight."

"I can cancel," Maggie said quickly, shooting her friend a *be quiet* look. "We were just getting together to discuss travel plans. It can wait until tomorrow."

"Why not bring him by?" Dan suggested. "I'm sure everyone would love to meet him. Not everyone in the political science department is like us and immersed in military studies. Some of our colleagues would get a real kick out of talking to a war hero."

Hunter and the men who'd likely determine the future of her career in the same room? It was insane. But she couldn't let Dan wine and dine Carter without her. She needed that job.

"Sounds great," she said. "What time? Can I bring anything?"

"Six, and you don't need to bring a thing," Dan said. "Look forward to meeting this war hero of yours."

"Dan?" A tall, leggy blonde who looked as if she spent every waking minute perfecting her appearance called from the nearby makeup counter. "We'll be late for lunch if we don't leave soon."

"My wife," he explained. "Gotta run. See you tonight."

"I thought your Ranger had plans for you tonight," Olivia muttered as Dan walked away.

"I'll have to take a rain check." The anticipation might drive her crazy, but she didn't have a choice. Everything she'd worked for was within her grasp. Fantasy sex would have to wait. "Carter has the power to decide my future. I need to be there."

"I take it Dan is your competition."

"Yes, but he hasn't published in years. Once I finish this book, I'll be more qualified. But my department is an old boys' club. If Carter throws his support behind Dan, others would likely follow his lead."

Maggie found her phone and dialed the number Hunter had given her.

"Chief Cross." His greeting sounded more like a salute.

"Hunter, it's Maggie. I need to take a rain check on tonight. We're going to a pool party."

"You can still wear your shoes."

"Not a chance. It's with my coworkers," Maggie said, taking the bag from the sales clerk. "I need to focus on work, and I'll need you on your best behavior."

"Done. But tomorrow night? You're mine."

BEER IN HAND, Hunter followed Maggie away from the folding table set up as a bar and around the pool. Their host, who'd greeted him with a used-car-salesman smile when they first arrived, owned a simple one-story colonial on a street just outside of town. The pool and the cement deck encompassed most of the backyard. Tiki torches stood in a line where the pool deck stopped and grass began.

Everything about the backyard screamed pool party—except Maggie. Tonight, she'd dressed the part of the responsible professor in her black slacks and white button-down shirt. He'd taken one look at her when she'd come down the stairs earlier and thought he'd mistaken "pool party" for "wake." But no, he'd arrived to find her fellow professors in shorts and T-shirts and their wives in sundresses. Some even wore bathing suits. And they all looked ready to party, everyone but Maggie.

The woman who'd turned down a wild night in bed to be here looked about as serious as a soldier locked and loaded for battle. He couldn't help himself. He leaned toward her, close enough to smell her sweet, soapy-clean scent, and dropped his voice. "I suppose now is not the time to tell you sex in an empty bedroom at your coworker's party is at the top of my fantasy list."

Without touching her, he felt the tension in her sky-rocket from a one to an off-the-charts fifteen. She stepped away from him. "No, I can't. Not here."

"Relax." He reached out to stop her from backing into a lit torch. "I wouldn't do that to you."

She eyed him suspiciously then turned her attention to the older gentleman walking toward them. "That's Professor Carter," she hissed. "Whoever he recommends for tenure will likely get it."

The old man bore a stronger resemblance to Santa Claus than any professor Hunter had ever seen. Then again, he'd joined the army at eighteen so he didn't know much about academics. But he'd pictured an old man in a tweed jacket with a hat, not a two-hundred-and-fifty-pound man in a Hawaiian shirt with a white beard.

"Margaret, what a surprise. I thought you would be too busy writing to attend," the older man said, grinning from ear to ear. "But I see you brought your book with you." The jolly professor turned to him and extended his free hand, the one not cradling what looked like three fingers of scotch. No wonder the man's nose was Rudolph-red.

"Gerry, this is Chief Hunter Cross with the U.S. Army Rangers," Maggie said. "Hunter, this is Professor Gerald Carter."

"Call me Gerry," he said, shaking Hunter's hand. "Must have done something amazing over there if Margaret wants to write about you. She's one smart cookie."

"She is," Hunter replied. He watched as Carter wrapped his arm around Maggie's waist, attempting to draw her closer. Maggie sidestepped, moving dangerously close to a tiki torch.

"Chief Cross is one of the soldiers who rode through Afghanistan."

"Ah, one of the cowboys," Carter said. He took a swig from his glass and closed in on Maggie. With her only escape blocked by a flaming torch, the drunk Santa impersonator caught Maggie around the waist.

Hunter waited for her to slap his hand away. Instead, she smiled and said, "They're not crazy about that moniker. Yes, they rode horses, but they are still soldiers. The interviews I've conducted so far have been fascinating. All the readers who raced out to buy the SEAL book will be lining up to learn about the Ranger's heroic mission."

Maggie rested her hand on his arm and tried to guide it away. Gerry didn't take the hint. Or maybe he thought she wanted his hand on her ass. Hunter watched Gerry's hand drift down to her lower back and dip below the waistline of her black pants.

Hunter studied Maggie, waiting for her to ask for his help. But she remained frozen in place, her body stiff as a board except for the hand holding a wineglass filled with seltzer. The fingers on that hand tapped the glass stem as if she was sending out a message in Morse code.

"Cowboys, soldiers—the man's a hero," Gerry said, raising his glass in Hunter's direction. "And your book sounds like a bestseller, Margaret. The college loves having bestselling authors in the classrooms," he added, giving her bottom a pat.

"Let's move away from the torches," Maggie suggested, stepping out of Gerry's reach. "I'm getting a little warm." She led them closer to the pool edge and positioned herself on the far side of Hunter.

"Better?" Hunter asked.

"Much." Maggie turned back to Gerry, who'd followed her like a dog chasing a bone. "I understand you're leaving on a cruise soon."

"Next week. After the tenure review board meeting," Gerry said. "I would love to see someone from the military studies area awarded tenure, which leaves you and Dan as the primary contenders for the job. But if you're writing a bestseller, the college would have a hard time turning you down. I can make that clear to them." Gerry inched closer to Maggie, seemingly oblivious to the fact that he might force Hunter into the pool. "Why don't you join me for a drink at the bar and tell me more about the book that is going to make you the youngest tenured professor in the political science department?"

One step away from doing a back flop into the water, Hunter decided he'd had enough. This man was drunk and determined to get his hands on Maggie. In his book that meant party time was over. Maybe she didn't want his help, but she was damn sure going to get it.

"Maggie, we need to be going," Hunter interrupted. "Remember you have that Skype date with Riley? I would hate for you to miss an interview. And this is the only time he can talk."

"A Skype session? Tonight?"

Hunter saw the confusion in her expression but plunged ahead, taking her by the arm and backing her away from Gerry's reach. "Yeah. You wanted to do a follow-up, right?"

He saw the precise moment her confusion gave way to a less flattering emotion. "Of course." She made a show of glancing at her watch and then up at Gerry with an apologetic expression. "I was so caught up in our little chat, I almost forgot to keep track of the time."

"That's what I'm here for," Hunter said.

"Lucky me," she muttered, pulling her arm free and stepping forward to kiss Gerry's cheek. To the jolly, groping professor, she said, "Thank you for your support, Gerry. It means so much to me."

Hunter reached out to reclaim her arm, but she sidestepped him. Pivoting on her heel, she headed for the path that ran alongside the house to the driveway. He followed.

MAGGIE MARCHED TO her car feeling as if her world was shifting beneath her feet. It was as if the gravel had turned to quicksand. She knew this feeling, remembered it from her childhood. Her control had slipped away at the worst possible moment.

"You could thank me now," Hunter said once they were both in the car. "That guy is a jerk."

Eyes narrowed, she turned to him, her hands gripping the steering wheel. "That jerk could make or break my career."

"He was all hands."

"I had the situation under control," Maggie ground out as she pulled onto the main road.

"I kept waiting for you to tell him to back off. When you didn't I thought I'd lend a hand. You can't expect me to stand by and do nothing."

"You should have let me handle him. I need Carter's support if I'm going to get tenure." The muscles in her shoulders tensed and she took the bend in the road a little too fast. Across from her, Hunter held on to the door. "If you hadn't made up some stupid excuse about an interview, which by the way made me look like a careless idiot for standing around drinking when I supposedly had work to do, I would have removed his wandering hands and kept the conversation focused on my book."

"You don't have to worry, Maggie. Good old Gerry is fascinated by your book. You already have his support."

"You can't know that for sure."

"I've worked with guys like him before. Unless he's trying to grab Dan's ass now, you have his vote. Trust me, Maggie."

She snorted. Trust him? The man had just railroaded her into walking away from an important conversation.

"You did last night," Hunter added.

She doubted she'd ever forget how it felt to stand at his mercy with her pants around her ankles. But she'd been acting out a fantasy. Tonight he'd messed with her reality.

"That's different. This is work. My future. You have no idea what this means to me."

"Then tell me," he said quietly.

Maggie turned down her long private drive and accelerated. When they reached the parking area in front of the house, she came to an abrupt stop and turned to face him.

"When I was younger, I worked so hard to keep our life moving forward. But at any moment it was like my father could pull the rug out from under me. Everyone at school thought I had my life together until he showed up drunk to meet with my teachers. All the bills were paid, until he decided to help but then forgot where he'd put the mail, and the electric company turned off our power. I can't live like that again."

"I'm not asking you to." Hunter reached out and took her hand. "Have a little faith in me. Not a lot, just a little."

Their interlaced fingers rested on the console between the seats. Maggie's gaze locked on their joined hands. She forced herself to relax for the first time since she'd set foot in Dan's backyard.

"I'll try," she said reluctantly. "As long as you don't pull another stunt like that."

"That's fair." Hunter nodded. "But next time, I expect you to stand up for yourself."

"I will." She hadn't wanted Carter's hands on her. But she was a big girl and could handle herself. She didn't need to be rescued. Of course, saving the day was Hunter's default. He was a hero—she just didn't need him to be hers.

He traced circles on the palm of her hand with his thumb. It felt as if he was brushing away her anger with his touch.

"I do trust you," she said. "To a point, but—"

"Enough for tomorrow night?" he asked.

Her throat went dry, but she managed an affirmative nod. Her mind went to the pair of heels in her closet. She'd known when she bought them that she wanted to follow him wherever he led her—when it came to sex. But she wasn't ready to let go of the rest of her life. She knew letting go in bed was only a temporary fix, like Saturday night. But she wasn't ready for more. She might never be.

14

MAGGIE WOKE UP before her alarm, and this time it wasn't the smell of coffee that had her marching down the stairs before six. She needed to write. Last night, Carter had suggested that a bestselling book would make her a shoo-in for tenure. Excitement coursed through her as she typed up her notes, crafting paragraph after paragraph about Hunter's mission on horseback. She stopped every so often to scribble follow-up questions.

Three hours into her work, Hunter appeared in the door with a mug. Maggie accepted the coffee with a smile, but remained focused on her computer screen. "Were the aid workers injured when you rescued them?"

"Good morning to you, too," he said.

Out of the corner of her eye, she saw him perch on the edge of her desk and fold his arms across his chest. Her mind might be focused on work, but her body? Every inch of her was aware of Hunter as a man, not a Ranger and the subject of her book. She sneaked a peek and her breath caught. A man without a shirt. Damn him. Desire pulsed through her.

"Well?" she asked, trying to keep her mind from following her body's let's-get-naked-with-him cues. "Were they? Injured?"

He hesitated, unfolding his arms and then crossing them again. "They'd taken a hit or two, but were still mobile."

"Did their limited mobility slow you down?" she asked, keeping her gaze locked on her computer.

"Is there a reason you won't look at me?"

"You're not wearing a shirt," she replied, her fingers moving over the keyboard.

"You've seen me without a shirt before," he said playfully.

"I'm working right now," she said. "We had a deal. We keep work and the other stuff separate."

Hunter chuckled. "The other stuff?"

Maggie felt a faint blush creep up her cheeks, but refused to turn away from her computer. It was too dangerous. If she looked again, she'd want to touch. And if she touched him…other stuff would happen. Here. On her desk. She crossed her legs, pressing her thighs together.

"You know what I'm talking about," she said.

"I do." Out of the corner of her eye, she saw him stand and move around behind her desk chair, disappearing from view. She felt his breath on her neck and then his lips brushed her skin. "But you have no idea what you're in for tonight, do you, Maggie? Only that you'll be completely under my control. And, honey, tonight we're playing out *my* fantasies."

Her hands froze on the keys.

"I'm going to town for a few supplies. Dinner will be at seven. Don't be late, and Maggie…?"

"Hmm?" she murmured, her body humming from the way his breath danced across the sensitive skin on the back of her neck.

"Be sure to wear your heels."

Maggie closed her eyes. There wasn't a flying chance in Hades she'd get her work done now. Still, she spent the rest of the afternoon pretending. Her mind kept drifting to the box of Jimmy Choos sitting on her bed. At five, she gave up and went upstairs to shower. She searched her closet for the simple black dress she'd bought for a cocktail party at the college. Not quite as sexy as the shoes, but better than her baggy suits and everyday sweats.

Two hours later, she followed the amazing smells down the stairs and found Hunter waiting for her with two champagne flutes at the bottom. He'd changed into a clean pair of jeans and a red polo, leaving her feeling overdressed.

His gaze ran down her body and settled on her feet. He looked back up at her, his eyes filled with sensual promise. "Love the shoes."

"Thanks," she said, pleased he liked her purchase. She took the glass from his hand. "You made dinner?"

He shook his head. "Reheated. Olive Garden."

Maggie sipped her champagne. She didn't have much practice with surprises, and not knowing what he had planned unnerved her. "I'm a little overdressed for the OG."

"You're perfect." He took her free hand. "Come with me."

Wobbling in her new shoes, Maggie followed him through to the kitchen, where he traded his champagne glass for a picnic hamper she hadn't used since she was a child. "Where did you find that?"

"In one of the storage closets beneath the stairs. I enlisted your housekeeper's help. And your gardener."

He'd asked her *gardener?* When he said fantasy, she thought he'd been talking about sex, not flowers. "You asked Fred for help? With what?"

"I'll show you."

He pushed through the side door and drew her out onto the stone path that ran around the house. Where the pavers stopped, a slate path began. It led through the clearing and disappeared into the wooded area.

"Fred said the slate had been in the garage for years," Hunter said. He gave her hand a tug, leading her onto the new path.

She nodded. "My dad bought them for a project he never started. I can't believe you did all this while I was working."

He shrugged, looking over his shoulder at her as he led her closer to the tree line. "Do you like it?"

She saw the apprehension in his eyes. This big, strong man who'd ridden a horse through a war zone wanted her approval. "I do. But I'm not sure I should follow you into the woods. Especially in these shoes."

"I'll catch you if you fall." His excitement was contagious, and she followed him into the dense wooded area, keeping her weight on her toes to prevent her heels from sinking. Behind them, the house disappeared from view. Maybe fifty yards in, they reached a clearing Maggie vaguely remembered from when she'd run around these woods as a very young child. A small round table that had been in her backyard, and the two matching chairs, sat beside what appeared to be a fire pit and a bale of hay. She turned to Hunter and raised an eyebrow. "This is your fantasy?"

"Patience, Miss Maggie. We'll get to that." He pointed to the hay bale. Beside it lay two sticks, a bag of marshmallows, a box of graham crackers and a pile of chocolate bars. "First, dinner and dessert."

"S'mores?"

"I figured, since you never really got to be a kid, you might have missed out on some of the best parts. There's nothing better than a perfectly toasted marshmallow with chocolate and graham crackers."

"Says the man who goes to car shows for the fake cheese."

"I'm serious, Maggie." He led her over to a chair and held it for her while she sat. "You need more fun in your life. You've been caring for yourself and others since what? Grade school?"

"I had my fun. On Saturday." The reminder of their first night together sparked between them.

"You don't just need to lose control in bed, honey." He smiled devilishly. "You need a s'more more than anyone I've ever met. But first, dinner."

Hunter unpacked the picnic hamper, pulling out bottles of sparkling water, piping hot breadsticks, a salad and two take-out containers. She peeked under the lid of one while he set up the plates and silverware. "Linguine Alfredo?"

"You said it was your favorite."

"I'm going to be too full after this meal for anything else." She felt her face flush at the thought of what he might have in store for her after dinner. Her imagination had been running wild ever since he'd sent her off to buy shoes. No matter what he had planned, she knew it would end with orgasms, and that sent a shiver of anticipation down her spine.

"We have all night," he said. "There's no rush."

Maggie relaxed in her chair and reached for a breadstick. The night air was warm, but not humid, and the sky was clear. In a few hours, the sun would sink behind the trees, leaving a sky full of stars. It was the perfect night for a picnic and campfire. The perfect night to set work aside and simply enjoy. They talked comfortably through the meal, moving to the hay bale for s'mores after Hunter built a fire in what Maggie assumed was record time.

"Have you done this before?" Hunter asked, handing her a stick.

She nodded. "Once with my grandfather, but not outside. We built a fire in the living room fireplace."

"It's been a long time. Maybe I should make your first one." He took her stick and put a marshmallow on it.

"You're experienced." She watched him turn the stick, careful to roast all sides. "Were you a Boy Scout?"

"No, Maggie. Not a Boy Scout." He used his free hand to snap a graham cracker in half and arrange a piece of chocolate on one side. Pulling his stick from the flame, he gently slid the marshmallow into the middle of his graham-cracker sandwich.

"Open your mouth."

She obeyed and he held the treat to her parted lips.

"Now bite."

She heard the snap of the cracker and tasted the warm milk chocolate mixed with gooey marshmallow. "It's perfect. Did you learn how to make these in the army?"

He smiled and offered her the rest. "I had a crush on this girl, and seeing as we weren't old enough to go out for dinner, I invited her over and we made s'mores. She didn't like the marshmallows, but she loved the chocolate."

"Would this be the same girl who broke your heart and sent you running from commitment?" she asked.

Hunter shook his head. "No one broke my heart."

"Then why do you run away from long term?"

He slid another marshmallow on his stick. "My job mostly. The lifestyle doesn't make relationships easy. My longest since I joined the Rangers clocks in at about four weeks, and I spent two of those weeks deployed without email or phone contact, so by the time I got around to sending my usual I-have-a-crazy-job-this-won't-work email from halfway around the world, she'd moved on. And I didn't have a great track record before that."

Maggie nodded. She'd known from the minute he'd said the word *Ranger* at the car show that his job was a personal relationship minefield. And right now, that sounded like a major plus. One more s'more and she might start to feel things for him she shouldn't.

"You really love it. Being a Ranger."

"Yeah. I like being where the action is. And I like being the best." He looked up from his marshmallow and smiled at her. "No matter what anyone tells you about those other Special Forces units, we're the most kick ass."

"But that doesn't mean you have to give up on the rest of your life. Some soldiers make it work," she said. "The relationship thing."

Hunter nodded. "They do. But I've got other commitments on my plate. Other people who need me."

Sierra popped into her mind, but she pushed away the questions. Not tonight. Not after he'd gone to all this trouble for her.

"Not everyone is as driven as you, Maggie." He turned the stick above the flame. "You never wanted to run away from your father's drinking and all that responsibility?"

"I did and I thought about it," she said. "But more than leaving, I wanted to stay and make things better."

"You certainly take on a lot." Hunter transferred the marshmallow to a chocolate-covered graham cracker and offered it to her. "You're a professor and you're writing your second book—"

"The first doesn't really count," Maggie interrupted. "It received great reviews, but no one outside of the military studies field bought it."

"Still counts. So you're writing your second book at what?"

"Twenty-eight." She took a bite of the s'more.

"And soon you'll be a tenured professor. That's a lot."

She looked at him in the soft campfire light. "Living with my dad was like riding a rickety roller coaster every day. You never knew when it was going to fall apart. I want a stable future. And that comes with responsibility."

Hunter leaned toward her, his hand resting on the hay bale beside her hip. His mouth touched hers and she felt his tongue lick the sticky sweet traces of chocolate and marshmallow from her lips. He kissed his way to her ear, sending delicious shivers down her body. "Not with me. With me, you set all that aside."

She inhaled sharply and closed her eyes, waiting for another kiss. She was ready to strip off her clothes and follow his orders right here on the hay bale. She waited, but heard only the sound of a chocolate bar wrapper.

Maggie opened her eyes and watched as he made a s'more for himself. He was teasing her. He knew his words would have her body burning with need and that there was nothing she could do about it. He was in control. It drove her crazy when he tried to take charge in her work life, but right now, under the stars? It thrilled her. She shifted, rubbing her inner thighs together, and watched him.

"What happened with the girl? The one who loved chocolate?"

"It didn't last. I was thirteen. She was fourteen. We were too young," he said. "But I scored a kiss."

"You went to all this trouble for a kiss?" she asked, licking her lips.

He leaned close again. "I want more than a kiss, Maggie, but not because I cooked for you. Because you want it, too."

Closing the gap, he licked her lips, and this time she tasted the chocolate on his tongue. She opened her mouth.

Reaching her hands up, she drew him into a slow, sweet kiss. She heard him drop the stick and felt his hands on the sides of her face, working their way into her hair, holding her still so his mouth and tongue could ravage her. When he pulled back, she felt a sharp pang of need for more.

"Are we there yet?" she murmured.

He raised an eyebrow, his hands still holding her. "Where?"

"The part I've been waiting for all night."

Hunter let out a tense laugh. "Hell, yes." His hands fell and he pushed himself up from the hay bale. "But not here."

He quickly extinguished the fire and reached for her. She took his hand and followed him back to the house as fast as her ridiculous heels would carry her. Her body hummed with excitement and nerves. After his romantic dinner in the woods, she didn't know what to expect from him. What kind of fantasies did a man who agreed to give a stranger amazing orgasms one day and make her s'mores the next have? And why the shoes?

Inside, he took her hand and led her down the hall to her guest room, currently his bedroom. She paused at the doorway. It was one thing to let a one-night lover take control in a hotel room, or to take off her clothes after too many margaritas, but sober in her guest room? It felt different. More intimate and risky even though she knew she was safe with him. Physically. The more she learned about him, the more time she spent with him, the more she worried that the sexual attraction between them might lead to something else. Something dangerous.

"Nervous?" he asked.

She nodded.

"Maggie, look at me."

She obeyed.

"Do you trust me not to hurt you?"

"Yes." She didn't have to think about it. Over the past few days this man, who in so many ways resembled the parent who'd nearly broken her faith in others, had earned her trust.

He drew her into the room, leaned over and whispered in her ear. "I'm going to make this good for you. Just relax and let me take control."

"I thought tonight was about what you want," she whispered.

"Honey, we're already halfway there. You. In those shoes. That's part of it." He took her hand and led her past the bed to the blue armchair by the window.

"And the other part?"

He sat down and looked up at her. "Take off your dress, but keep the shoes."

Maggie stared at him. The orange glow from the setting sun poured in the open window, and in the distance she heard the soft sound of crickets. Could she do this? Strip while he sat and watched?

"You don't have to think about it, Maggie. Not in here. Not with me."

She reached her arms behind her and found the zipper. She wanted to do this, she realized. He'd given her what she wanted that first night. If this was his fantasy, she'd do everything she could to make it good for him.

Slowly, she drew the zipper down her back. Reaching up to her shoulders, she started to peel off the dress, revealing the new black lace bra Olivia had insisted she purchase to match her shoes. She shimmied the fabric over her hips and let it fall to the floor. Stepping aside, she waited for his next order.

"Take off your bra and panties."

Maggie stripped away her underwear until she stood in

front of him in only her heels. This might be his fantasy, but she was more turned on than she'd ever been. Her skin ached for his touch, his mouth.

"Come here," he commanded. She obeyed, his words sending a shiver of desire racing through her and settling in her core.

He took her hand and pulled her forward until she stood between his splayed thighs. "Kneel down, Maggie."

She sank to the floor, her knees pressing into the plush carpet. He guided her hand to his zipper and she understood what he wanted. Slowly, she freed him from his pants and boxers. She glanced up at him and he nodded, his expression tight, as if he needed this too much to say another word. Closing her eyes, she bent her head and took him in her mouth.

HUNTER'S MIND BLANKED. His world at this moment was Maggie's mouth on him, the feel of her lips, her tongue and her hand wrapped around him. Eyes open, he watched her, running his gaze down her naked body to her sexy black heels. God, those shoes really did it for him.

"I'm close, Maggie," he rasped.

She made a purring sound in the back of her throat that pushed him right over the edge. He held her head in his hands as his hips lifted off the chair. He thrust up into her mouth, forcing her to take him as deeply as she could. Without taking his eyes off her, he exploded. Pleasure rocked him from head to toe.

As his orgasm eased and faded, he closed his eyes. More than a few women had serviced him like this. Well, maybe not exactly like this. Naked except for the supersexy shoes was a first. But he'd never felt this warm afterglow.

Opening his eyes, he looked down at Maggie's expectant expression. "Come here," he said, drawing her up onto his lap. He wrapped his arms around her, cradling her head against his chest.

"That was your fantasy?" she asked quietly.

"Yeah. Not very original, huh?"

"It really worked for me. I don't think I've ever felt so wildly sexy and powerful at the same time." Her voice was so soft against his shirt he barely heard her. He felt her fingers unbuttoning his polo and then her lips against his bare skin. He might have had his orgasm, but she still needed hers.

"I promised I'd take care of you." He gently pushed her off his lap, immediately missing the feel of her pressed against him. "Let's go to bed, Maggie."

With his hands on her hips, he guided her back until she hit the edge of the bed. Before she fell onto her back, he said, "Turn around."

She followed his orders, bending at the waist and resting her forearms on the cream-colored comforter.

"Stretch your arms out over your head," he commanded. "That's it. Palms flat. Good girl." He stroked one hand from the nape of her neck down to her raised bottom. She groaned, pushing back against him. He lightly swatted her bottom. "I didn't tell you to move."

"Not rough," she said, her voice muffled by the comforter on the bed.

"That didn't hurt, Maggie." He ran his hand over her bottom and down between her legs. "I think it turned you on."

"Please," she whimpered as his fingers glided over her most sensitive spot.

"Patience, Miss Maggie." He walked around the side of the bed stark naked and retrieved the box of condoms he'd placed in the night table earlier. Condom in hand, he moved back until he stood behind her. Allowing his body time to recover, he kissed her senseless, running his mouth down her spine.

"Spread your legs wider." He dropped to his knees, adjusting his position until his tongue lapped at the spot guaranteed to have her crying his name. He wanted to hear her calling out for him, acknowledging that he was the one to push her over the edge.

She hadn't lied when she said his fantasy worked for her. It didn't take long for her to moan and quiver with pleasure. He stayed with her until her first orgasm faded. When she was wet and begging for another, he stood, covered himself and entered her.

The motions were familiar, but something was different this time. His last clear thought before he lost himself in the pleasure? This wasn't just sex. Not for him. He was making love to her with everything he had.

He reached forward, wrapped his hand in her hair and pulled back until he could see her face. She looked beautiful, her lips swollen, her eyes wild with need. "I'm never going to get enough of you, am I?"

He released her hair, shifting his grip to her hips as he slammed into her again and again. When it was over, he'd probably worry about what it all meant. But right now? Inside her? It felt right.

Seconds later, he felt her tighten around him and he couldn't wait any longer. He exploded. His mind blanked. Pleasure rocked him from head to toe. And Maggie, beautiful, sexy, determined Maggie, was right there with him, screaming out his name as she beat the palm of her hand against the bed.

Spent, but feeling better than he had in months, he withdrew from her. "Lie down, honey," he commanded as he cleaned himself up. Maggie obeyed, rolling to her side, her high heels hanging off the bed. Hunter lay down beside her, with her back nestled against the front of his body. With her bottom pressed against him, he'd be ready for round three soon.

As if she'd read his mind and had other plans, Maggie rolled to her back and looked up at him. "I should go."

"Go where? You live here." He propped his head up with his right hand while the left brushed a strand of hair from her face.

She smiled up at him. "Back to my room."

"Stay," he said. "Spend the night with me."

"We're flying to Tennessee tomorrow. I need to get ready."

"You'll have time in the morning." He'd never begged a woman to stay the night. Not that he was down on his hands and knees now, but he felt damn close. He should be grateful she wanted to leave. Spending the night together inched the business-by-day/sex-by-night thing they had going straight into relationship territory.

"Hunter, it's not a good idea," she said softly.

His fingers ran down her throat until he found her collarbone. "I know, honey. We're not a good idea. I'm a long way from being ready for commitment and you need stability in your life more than anyone I've ever met. But there's one place where we work, where I'm just what you need, and that's right here in this bed. Stay with me, Maggie."

"I can't." She reached up and caught his hand in hers. Slowly, she pushed it away as she sat up. "I'm sorry. I can't stay here."

Hunter watched her pick up her dress, pull it on and walk away. Maybe she was right. Spending the night would lead to feelings he couldn't afford.

15

FOR THE SECOND DAY in a row, Maggie woke up before her alarm clock. Only today, a loud banging forced her eyes open. It sounded as if Hunter had decided to use a mallet on her bedroom door. Maggie pushed back the covers and found her slippers.

"I'm coming." She shuffled across her room and opened the door expecting to find Hunter holding a hammer and a cup of coffee on the other side. Instead, she found an empty hall.

"Hunter?"

The hammering started again. Now that she was awake, she realized the sound was coming from outside. Maggie headed down the stairs to the kitchen. First stop, caffeine, and then she would find the source of the sound that had driven her out of bed at—she glanced at her watch—seven in the morning.

The welcome smell of French roast greeted her as she pushed through the swinging door. Hunter must be awake. But if he was up, why hadn't he put a stop to the horrible banging noises? Maggie filled the mug set out beside the coffeemaker and headed for the side door leading to the yard. There was only one explanation.

She found Hunter on a ladder, hammer in hand, beating a piece of metal fifteen or so feet from her bedroom windows. He wore a pair of ripped jeans and a gray T-shirt that clung to his sweaty body. Even two stories down on the ground, she could see his biceps bulge as he swung the hammer. Her pulse raced at the sight, remembering what that body had done to her last night.

"What are you doing?" she asked.

"Good morning." He set down the hammer and smiled at her. "I was up early so I thought I'd fix your gutters. They were overflowing the other night. After the storm." He began climbing down the ladder. "At first, I thought they needed to be cleaned, but when I got up here I saw they were bent out of shape. I think a tree branch might have hit them."

Maggie frowned. She'd gone to bed unsettled last night. It wasn't the sex, but the way he'd asked her to stay. Spending the night with a man she was head over heels in lust with felt dangerous—not physically, but emotionally. She'd comforted herself with the fact that he knew he was wrong for her. But now, as she watched him repair her home, the unsettled feeling returned.

"I have someone who is paid to maintain those," she said.

"You should fire him. He's doing a shitty job if he let them get to this point. You really should replace them. If I had more time here, I'd offer to do it. Though I've got them mostly fixed, now."

Maggie sipped her coffee, forcing her fingers to remain still. He was doing her a favor. She should be thanking him. But she couldn't find the words. This was her house. She'd been taking care of it for nearly two decades.

"What time were you up?" she asked.

He shrugged as he stepped off the ladder. "I couldn't sleep last night. I started up here around five-thirty or six."

"You didn't have to do this."

Hunter cocked his head to one side and studied her. "It bothers you, doesn't it?"

"Yes," she said, looking down at her mug. "It's not that I don't appreciate it. I do. I am simply accustomed to taking care of the house on my own. Just because we're sleeping together doesn't mean you need to fix my gutters."

Hunter shook his head. "Whether you like it or not, we're more than two people who work together and have sex. We're friends, Maggie. Or at least I thought we were." He turned and started to walk away.

"Hunter," Maggie called after him.

He glanced over his shoulder. "I'm going for a run. I need to get some exercise before we leave for the airport. I'll put the ladder away when I get back, if that's all right with you."

Maggie nodded and watched him walk away. She should have hidden her unease, said a quick thank you and walked away. It wasn't his fault she needed to control every little part of her life. She was learning to let go in bed with him, but when it came to the rest of her life? Maybe one day, but not yet.

An hour later, Maggie sat at her desk reviewing her list of questions for Hunter's teammates when the doorbell buzzed. Had Hunter forgotten his key? The buzzer rang a second time. Frowning, she stood and went to get the door. It had better be Hunter. Still wearing her pajamas and robe, she wasn't dressed for company. She was halfway to the door before it occurred to her that her ex-fiancé might be on her front porch.

If Derrick had decided to show up again, she'd drive to the police station right after she kicked him out and put on some clothes. She'd request a restraining order. Maybe Hunter had been right. Rejection could turn a previously sane man into a low-fat-muffin-wielding stalker.

Peering through the peephole, Maggie saw a tall, model-thin brunette.

Or maybe Derrick had received the message loud and clear, and now one of Hunter's exes had decided to grace her doorstep. Of course, there was always the possibility Little Miss I-only-eat-rice-cakes thought she was Hunter's current girlfriend. Maybe trusting him had been one massive mistake.

"Hi, can I help you?" Maggie asked, opening the door just a crack. Not that this woman was dressed to impress. Far from it, in fact. Her cutoff jean shorts looked as if she hadn't washed them in weeks, and her fitted black T-shirt appeared slept in. Maggie glanced over her unexpected guest's shoulder and saw a beat-up white pickup that would probably be more at home in the junkyard than her driveway.

The woman shifted from one foot to the other. Nerves? No, this woman seemed jittery, almost as if she might start shaking uncontrollably right there on Maggie's front steps.

"I'm looking for Hunter."

Big surprise there.

"He's not here at the moment. But I can tell him you stopped by." Maggie paused, but the other woman just furrowed her brow. "And you are?"

"Sierra."

Just like that the bubble burst on her fantasy. Her knuckles turned white as she gripped the door. She should have asked about his mystery woman before last night. But why should she care? She'd only wanted one more night with Hunter, and now that Sierra had arrived, she wouldn't be tempted to ask for another, she told herself. Still, the dread lingered.

"I'm his sister," Sierra said, her voice clear despite her jumpy movements. "He probably didn't mention me, but I really need to talk to him. Is there any chance I could wait for him? I can sit in my car—"

"No, please come in." Maggie stepped back and swung the door open, no longer caring about her attire as the puzzle pieces surrounding her morning visitor's identity fell into place, and relief swept her from head to toe. His sister. Not his lover or his girlfriend.

Watching Sierra closely, Maggie had a hunch Hunter's sister needed the money and doctors she'd overheard him talking about on the phone. Recovering alcoholics and drug users often experienced jitters and shaking after they quit. Assuming Sierra was sober. Leaving rehab early? Not a good sign.

Maggie led the younger woman down the hall and through the swinging door. "Can I get you something? Coffee? Tea? Water?"

Sierra scanned the kitchen, shaking her head. "I'm okay."

No, you're not. Maggie bit back the words.

"Would you like to sit down? I was just about to make breakfast, which for me involves opening a cereal box, but you're welcome to a bowl. I also have muffins." Maggie had an overwhelming urge to feed the shaking, stick-thin girl.

Sierra nodded, but stopped short of verbally committing to anything. "When do you expect Hunter will be back?"

"Soon. Ten minutes, maybe." Maggie retrieved the leftover muffins from the breadbox and set them on a plate. She opened the fridge and pulled out butter and milk. Then she turned to face Hunter's sister. Maggie hesitated a moment, but her curiosity won. "So you're in rehab? That's a big step. Congratulations."

Sierra looked like a frightened deer with an open wound, caught but unable to escape. The silence stretched until it bordered on awkward.

"I admire your courage." Maggie took one of the blueberry muffins her housekeeper had dropped off yesterday, cut it in half and smeared it with butter, hoping Sierra would follow her lead. "I tried for years to get my dad to seek treatment, but he always had an excuse."

"Your dad," Sierra repeated, selecting a bran muffin.

"He drank." Maggie turned to the sink and filled two glasses with water. She passed one across the island to Hunter's sister.

Sierra looked straight at Maggie, her gaze filled with understanding. "I'm sorry."

Maggie nodded and fought the urge to hug Sierra. She could count on one hand the number of people she'd told about her father's drinking, and of those very few understood what addiction did to a person. They ate in silence, Sierra's eyes turning to the door every few seconds. Clearly Hunter's sister didn't feel the instant bond between them that Maggie did.

"Hunter will be back soon," she said. "But he'll probably be wondering why you left rehab."

"I couldn't stay there any longer." Sierra spoke in a strong, clear voice. "I couldn't let Hunter spend every penny he has on me. He's already spent his entire savings on my recovery. I'm grateful, believe me, I am, but any more is just too much of a burden."

"I'm sure Hunter feels having you sober is worth the cost," Maggie said.

Sierra broke the muffin into pieces as if she couldn't

speak without moving some part of her body. Nervous hands. Maggie could relate.

"Now that I'm clean I understand how selfish I was, ignoring my family and friends when they tried to help, forcing them to deal with my problems when they had their own to manage."

Maggie nodded. Sierra sounded like a walking, talking rehab brochure—and Maggie would know. She'd read them all at some point while trying to convince her father to seek help, but something about Sierra's voice suggested sincerity.

"I'm not going to start using again," Sierra continued. "Another month of rehab won't change that."

"It might help you stay clean," Maggie said.

"I can do this. I'm going to get my life back on track. I've changed. And this time, I'm not going to let Hunter down. Or myself."

God, how Maggie had longed to hear those words from her father, for him to wake up from his drunken haze and admit how destructive his drinking was. Oh, he'd apologized plenty, but he'd never meant it. He'd never tried to change. If he'd only had an ounce of Sierra's determination.

"Sierra, I know you believe you can stay clean without rehab, but if the doctors think you should still be there, maybe you should be selfish for a little longer." Maggie walked around the island and pulled out the chair beside Hunter's sister.

"He can't pay for it," Sierra said bluntly. "He's already past due on last month's bill. I know. I broke into the office and saw the second delinquent notice when I was looking for his temporary address. Your address."

Maggie reached over, covering Sierra's hand with hers. "Breaking and entering really isn't the first sign of recovery."

"I had to find Hunter."

The kitchen door swung open and a sweaty, shirtless Hunter strode into the room. "You found me. Now, do you mind telling me what the hell you're doing here?"

HUNTER HAD RUN the last mile back to the house driven by one thought. Shower sex. He'd raced down the hall planning to scoop Maggie up, carry her to the first floor guest bathroom and make her forget all about her gutters. Instead, he'd found her perched on a kitchen stool beside his sister. He glanced out the window over the sink. How had he missed Sierra's piece-of-shit truck parked beside the Mercedes? Shower sex. He'd been too damn focused on getting Maggie naked and under running water.

"Well, Sierra?" he demanded, hands on hips. His chest still heaved from exertion. Pile on a heavy dose of what-the-hell-is-my-sister-doing-here anger and he didn't even trust himself to pour a glass of water. He just might smash the damn thing on the floor.

Sierra let go of Maggie's hand and straightened her spine as if she'd prepared for this confrontation. Smart girl. She'd known he'd be pissed.

"I know what you're thinking, but I'm clean now and I'm not going to start again."

"Just because you aren't using now doesn't mean you won't use again later," Hunter challenged. "You should be in rehab. The doctors said you needed to be there."

Sierra shook her head. "I can do this. Stay sober. I know I can. If you can just let me crash at your place in Tennessee until I find a job, I can get back on my feet. Please, Hunter, you've done enough. It's time for me to take care of myself. Once I have a job, I can get a place of my own. So if I can just stay—"

"No, you can't." He went over to the cabinet, took out

a glass and turned on the faucet, too damn thirsty to wait
any longer.

"Please, it won't be for long," Sierra pleaded.

Without turning around, he took a long drink. The water
solved the problem of his thirst, but it didn't change what
he had to tell Sierra and, because she was still in the room,
Maggie. "I don't have a place anymore."

No one said a word, but he knew they were thinking
the same thing he was. He didn't have a home because he
was flat broke. He couldn't even afford to keep a roof over
his sister's head. Yeah, she should have stayed in rehab,
but that didn't change the fact that when she eventually
did get out, he still wouldn't have a place for her to sleep
while she rebuilt her life. Sierra was his sister, his family.
She meant more to him than anything in the world—his
job, his pride, anything—and he had no way to take care
of her, not without money. He had nothing to give either
of these women.

Hunter glanced at Maggie. He could tell himself he
only wanted kinky sex with her until he was blue in the
face. After last night, he knew the truth. A week with her
wasn't enough. He wanted her in his life. But he couldn't
start a relationship when he had no way to take care of her.

Hunter closed his eyes and mentally set aside his pride.
He'd beg if he had to, but he wasn't letting his sister walk
away from her recovery. "I don't have a place right now,"
he clarified. "But I'll have somewhere for you to stay soon.
And right now, you need to go back to rehab."

"I can't," Sierra said. "It's too expensive."

"Sierra—"

"I'll pay for it," Maggie interrupted.

Silence filled the kitchen as Hunter turned his attention to Maggie. She looked determined, just as she had
that day he'd watched her present her book to a room full

of generals. Hunter shook his head. "Maggie, I can't ask you to do that."

"I'm offering," she said. "I have the money."

"Sierra's my family. Helping her is my responsibility."

"I know all about responsibility. I've been buried under it most of my life. Sometimes you have to ask for help."

Hunter snorted. "Yeah, you're great at that. You nearly bit off my head earlier for fixing your gutters."

"I didn't say I was good at it, but I'm getting better," she said, offering the faintest hint of a smile before her expression turned serious again. "Please, Hunter, let me do this. Not just for you, for your sister."

Hunter watched as Maggie reached over and placed her hand over Sierra's.

"If money had been the only thing standing between my father and sobriety, I would have done anything and everything to get it, even if it meant accepting someone's help." Maggie turned to Sierra. "I want to help you. I admire your determination. That was something my father never had, and no amount of pushing on my part could change that. Please, Sierra. It would mean a lot to me."

"Thank you," Sierra said, slowly withdrawing her hand from Maggie's. "But my brother's right. We can't take your money."

"There's another way," Hunter said. "I was offered a private security job. It pays well. I'll give them a call and see if the offer still stands."

"You'd leave the job you love instead of taking my money?" Maggie asked.

"The work might not be that different." He'd told the company a flat-out no without getting the details. But whether they shipped him off to a war zone or kept him stateside, it wouldn't be the end of the world.

"No," Maggie insisted. She turned to Sierra. "I'll give

it to you as a loan. You can pay me back. Whenever you're ready."

A loan. The last thing he needed was another IOU, and he damn sure wasn't going to saddle Sierra with the burden, not when she needed to focus on staying sober. "Sierra, can you give us a minute?"

His sister nodded. "Sure."

"You can wait on the porch," he said. Once his sister was out of earshot, he rested his hands on the island and looked at Maggie. "Why are you doing this, Maggie?"

"Because we're friends. I can't fix your gutters, but I can do this. After you leave and I finish my book, after the sexual part of our relationship ends, I like to think that we will remain friends. This is what friends do for each other, isn't it?"

Hunter ran his hand through his hair and looked away. "Christ, Maggie, you don't understand. Her treatment is expensive. It's taking nearly all I have and then some right now. It could be years before I can repay you. I have a mountain of debt. This isn't the first time Sierra has needed money."

"Then I'll wait," she said. "Hunter, look at me." He turned to her and saw the open honesty in her eyes. "Please. Let me do this. I couldn't save my father. But Sierra? I can help her. I want to help her. Not just for you, but because she deserves a chance to stay sober. Please, let me pay for it."

"Maggie, I want you to understand, I will repay every cent. I promise you."

"I believe you." Maggie smiled. "I know you don't break your promises."

"Good. As long as we're clear. This is a loan. Let's tell Sierra the good news. And then get her the hell out of here and back to rehab so I can thank you properly."

"More s'mores?"

"What I have in mind involves your guest room shower," he said.

Maggie smiled at him, her eyes lighting up with that intoxicating mix of boldness and innocence. That look—it hit him square in the gut. The thrill he found when jumping out of a helo with his team? It didn't compare to the rush he got from being with Maggie. That twinge he'd felt when she walked away last Saturday had grown into something more, something that threatened to march him straight into relationship territory.

He'd fallen for her. As it stood now, he'd fallen so far he couldn't settle for being the guy she turned to for orgasms, to fulfill her fantasies. He needed the promise that she'd be there for him the next day and the day after that. He wanted to be the man she woke up to, not the one she walked away from after sex. Hell, he'd had a better time last night sharing s'mores on a bale of hay than he'd ever had working as a Ranger. He didn't need his job, a promotion or a pay raise. What he needed was standing right in front of him. Maggie.

With her, a relationship wasn't about what he had to give, it was about taking care of each other. She could help him provide for his family and he could offer her the stability she needed. He could be the person she trusted.

Hunter frowned as he followed Maggie through the swinging door. What he wanted didn't matter if she didn't trust him. Maggie had serious control issues. She might fantasize about letting someone else take the lead, about letting another person into her life, but in reality, it was hard for her to trust. And if she ever found out he'd withheld information for her book? She'd run for the door.

He wasn't going to let that happen.

16

AT EIGHT THAT EVENING, they pulled into the parking lot at the Guest Suites hotel a few miles down the road from Fort Campbell. Maggie had kept her gaze focused out the window, taking in the local sites—the quaint Clarksville downtown, the local bars and, as they passed over a bridge, the Red River.

Hunter put the car in Park and turned to her. "Sure you're ready for tomorrow?"

Maggie nodded. They'd spent the entire flight to Tennessee talking about her interviews with his teammates. For the first time since they'd started working together, he'd answered all of her questions, telling her everything he could about the men she would meet in the morning. He'd told her how to put them at ease, what questions each man could answer for her and what questions might make them nervous and clam up. "Thanks to you, I'm more ready than I've ever been for an interview."

Hunter smiled. "Good. That's good."

Maggie reached for the passenger-side door, but something, maybe it was lust, or maybe she'd simply grown accustomed to having him around, made her pause and turn to him. "Would you like to come up?"

His smile faded. "I'm okay, Maggie. I called one of my buddies. I'm going to crash on his couch tonight. I'll meet you for breakfast and drive you over to the base."

"I wasn't asking you because I didn't think you had anyplace else to go," she said. "I'm asking because I want you to come up." She wanted one more night with him, one last chance to live out her fantasies. After she interviewed his teammates, his role as her liaison would end. Sure, he'd asked to read her rough drafts, but that could all be done long distance, over email. He was a highly trained soldier; the army couldn't afford to keep him in upstate New York for more than a week, not when he could be off fighting the bad guys. She'd known when she'd stepped on the plane this afternoon that she would be flying back alone.

Even if their work wasn't keeping them in separate states, Hunter had made it clear he was not interested in anything long term. And if he changed his mind? It still wouldn't work. She needed stability and control. She couldn't handle a head-over-heels love affair.

But maybe she was ready to spend the night with him. One night in his bed. She could do that without panicking, couldn't she?

"Please," she added.

"Maggie, if I come up, I'm staying the night."

She nodded. "I know. Just promise me we won't get too much sleep."

Hunter leaned over and brushed his lips across hers. His hand reached up and caressed her face. "Honey, that's one promise I can keep."

HUNTER LED THE way from the parking lot to the check-in desk, waiting patiently with the bags while Maggie retrieved her room key. He knew she'd invited him up because she thought this would be their last night together.

She would fly back to New York tomorrow afternoon after she met with his teammates. She thought that was the end. But it wasn't. Not if he had his way. He planned on telling her how he felt about her before she left. And when he did, he hoped like hell that when she flew home, things wouldn't end between them.

He was willing to do whatever it took to keep her in his life. Sure, his job was a bitch when it came to relationships, but this time he'd make it work. He didn't have a choice. He needed her in his life. He wanted to come home to her. At the end of the day, that mattered more than damn near anything else. Once he shared his feelings with her, how could she walk away forever?

They were more than bed-pounding sex. She had to know that by now. Not that he wanted the off-the-charts sparks between them to simmer down. Hell, just the opposite.

Hunter grinned like a fool, nodding to an elderly couple passing through the lobby. He'd tell her how he felt, all right. But first, he'd show her.

When Maggie returned with the keys, he picked up their bags and followed her to their ground floor suite. The hotel wasn't as fancy as the Marriott near West Point. Everything about the room was generic from the desk to the white robes hanging on the outside of the door to the bathroom—everything but the queen-size four-poster bed.

Hunter took Maggie's bag from her and wheeled it aside. Then he leaned forward and brushed his lips over hers, offering a soft, gentle promise before he pulled back. He'd take this slow even if it killed him, learning and fulfilling Maggie's every desire and need. When he was done, there would be no doubt in her mind that he was the man for her.

"I want to take care of you," he whispered against her lips. "All of you. I want to make your dreams come true."

"Hunter," she murmured.

He kept the kisses light and playful, gliding his tongue along her lips and then withdrawing when she opened her mouth against his. He felt Maggie's hands under his shirt, moving up his back, drawing his body closer to hers as he kissed a trail down her jaw.

His mouth found the place on her neck that drove her wild as his hands ran over her waist and up under the front of her T-shirt. Taking his time, he teased the erogenous area, before drifting down to her shoulder then back to her neck. Maggie whimpered in his arms and he repeated the move.

While his lips worshipped her soft, soapy-sweet-smelling skin, his fingers glided up and down her torso, brushing the fabric of her bra before drifting lower again. When he couldn't wait any longer, he drew her clothing up, pausing briefly to cup his hands over her breasts.

"Lift your arms," he said softly, his lips never breaking contact with the back of her neck. His command sounded more as though he was begging than demanding, but he didn't care. Maybe it was the sweet smell of her hair or the softness of her skin, but all he could think about was Maggie. Naked. Now.

Command or not, she obeyed, raising her arms up even though he could feel her body turning to jelly the more he kissed her sensitive neck. Stepping back, he pulled her shirt over her head and tossed it aside while Maggie fumbled with the waistband of her pants.

"Too many clothes," she muttered, stripping off her underwear and tossing it on top of her skirt.

"Couldn't agree more." Without taking his eyes off her as she deftly removed her bra, he shed his clothes in record time, not caring if he ever found them. But Little Miss Maggie didn't make a run for the bed. Instead, she turned to face him, and with that brazen glint in her eyes he remembered oh-so-well from their first night together, dropped to her knees, her mouth inches from his erection.

"Maggie," he managed, his voice hoarse with anticipation. God, he wanted her, too, but tonight was about her.

"Please. I want to taste you." Her lips hovered so close he felt her breath as a few drops of liquid spilled from him. And then she wrapped her lips around him.

Hunter closed his eyes and refocused on his self-control, driving away the I'm-going-to-come-now urge. He wasn't a teenager, and this wasn't some supersmart high school senior he'd taken for a ride in his mother's car. He wanted this woman now, tomorrow and the next day.

Opening his eyes, he watched her tongue run up from the base of his erection to the tip. His body told him he couldn't take much more of her teasing.

"Maggie, I like this. Hell, you know I love it," he gasped. "But I can't take much more. When I come, I want to be inside you, face-to-face, watching you come with me."

She gave him one last kiss before pulling back and looking up at him. "Right here?"

"On the bed."

He watched her rise and back away from him slowly. When her legs hit the bed, she let herself fall. Propping herself up on her elbows, she looked at him with a hint of hesitation in her eyes. "Are you coming?"

Hell, yes. But that brief glimpse of oh-my-God-am-I-doing-this-right in her gaze kept him from pouncing and burying himself inside her. When he entered her, he wanted her to be out of her mind with need, so focused on her own primal wants that she couldn't second-guess herself. And he knew just how to get her there. He knew how to blow her fantasies out of the water.

Taking a step back, he searched for his clothes, bent

over and pulled a condom out of his pocket, tossing it on the bed beside her. "For later."

"Just one?"

"To start. But we're not there yet." Reaching for the hotel robe hanging on the bathroom door, he pulled the belt free. He smiled, letting his eyelids lower slightly.

"Do you trust me, Maggie?"

MAGGIE COULDN'T TAKE her eyes off the white sash in his hands. Her thighs clenched at the thought of what he might do with his makeshift rope. Bind her hands? Her feet? Strap her to the bed and take control of her body? The images set her need on edge.

But it all came down to trust. Did she trust him with her body? Yes. Her desire demanded it. Still, she hesitated. Did she trust herself not to panic when he restrained her? Could she give herself to him physically and keep her emotions in check, the ones that sent her into panic when she lost control?

"Maggie?"

"Yes," she said simply. Hunter lunged before her lips had even closed around the word. He moved like a warrior intent on his prey. A visibly aroused, naked warrior.

Hovering over her, the sash pulled taut between his fists, he smiled wickedly. "I'm going to tie you up now."

She'd never thought those words would feel like a caress on her skin, but her nipples hardened in response and she felt herself growing impossibly wet. She'd made the right choice. She wanted this.

"Hold out your arms."

Maggie obeyed, letting her body fall back onto the down comforter. He moved onto the bed, straddling her abdomen, one knee on either side of her as he quickly and expertly bound her wrists together. Sash in one hand, he supported his upper body with the other, and as he leaned forward, he drew her arms up. She couldn't see anything but Hunter, the stubble on his chin, the tension in his toned chest, and lower down the hardness she'd tasted earlier, but she heard the swish of the fabric as he tied her to the bedpost.

He pulled back, still kneeling over her. His gaze ran down from her hands to her breasts and his eyes narrowed, lips parted. Heaven help her, he looked like a man on a mission.

"Hunter?" Now that he had her here, at his mercy, what did he intend to do? She tried to lift her arms, tugging at the bonds. He'd left her barely an inch of leeway.

"Trust me, Maggie," he said, his voice rough and low. "I'm going to take care of you."

He leaned forward again, and for a second she wondered if he meant to loosen the sash a bit to reassure her, but then she felt his lips brush her arms, his tongue slip under the binding to graze her wrists. Her body writhed beneath him, her hesitation replaced with lust.

Slowly, he kissed a gentle trail down to her right elbow. He began to kiss, suck and explore the bend in her arm, making her breasts ache for his mouth. Arching up, she prayed he'd take the hint, but no, he remained focused on her arm.

Just when she thought she might scream *kiss me lower,* he shifted his weight back, hovering over her, close enough for his erection to brush her stomach. Finally, *finally,* he touched her breast, shock waves radiating from her sensitive skin.

But as quickly as he touched her, he stole his hand away, dropping his mouth to her collarbone.

"Lower," she begged, her voice hoarse with need.

"Not yet, Maggie," he murmured against her skin. "Not yet."

Minutes felt like hours as he kissed his way around and between her breasts, not once claiming her hardened nipples. Her body burned, arching and squirming beneath him. Every time his erection touched her belly, her hips shifted, pushing up as if trying to capture him. She planted her feet on the bed, to better lift her hips, but his weight thwarted her attempts. With her hands bound overhead, she had no choice but to wait.

He drew one nipple into his mouth. Maggie moaned, her body spiraling out of control. Madness—he'd driven her to the brink of insanity, for her desire was so intense.

"I never want this to end," he said, his mouth hovering over her chest. "But I can't wait much longer."

Hunter shifted farther down her and retrieved the foil packet from the mattress. He covered himself, spreading her gently with one hand. Slowly, he guided himself inside her with his other, taking his time, letting her feel every inch as he penetrated her. Her core tightened around him, and she silently begged him never to leave. Still, he slid out and waited a beat before thrusting back in.

He moved slowly as if he wanted to hold her orgasm at bay until dawn, but then he thrust deeper, harder, faster, as if he'd found the rhythm he'd been searching for.

Who knew the missionary position could be so exciting? Sensations rippled up like little pre-orgasmic shock waves. If this were only the beginning, what would happen to her body when she came?

Hunter leaned forward until his chest pressed against hers. His hips continued to tilt and thrust deep within her, and she didn't have to wonder anymore.

Wave after wave of pure, indescribable pleasure washed

over her. She tingled, then shattered from her bound hands, to her elbows, to the tips of her toes.

Carnal. Raw. Tied-to-the-bed bliss.

When she came down, slowly drifting back to the present as if the power of her orgasm had taken her someplace far away, she knew she'd found what she'd been searching for that night at the car show. Deep inside, secretly, she'd craved this passion, this ability to hand herself over to a man and trust he would take care of her needs.

"Maggie," he groaned. Above her, Hunter gasped, pushing into her one final time. She opened her eyes and watched his body tense and shudder. He lowered his head until his forehead rested against hers. His breathing was ragged, as if he'd just run a marathon.

"Hell, Maggie," he moaned as he rolled off her and collapsed on the bed beside her.

"Hunter?" she said, pulling at the binding holding her hands above her head. Now that the lust had passed and the aftershocks of her orgasm faded, she felt less and less comfortable tied to the bed.

"I need a minute," Hunter said. "Maybe ten."

"Could you untie me first?"

He reached up and tugged on the binding. "You're free."

"Thank you," she murmured. But the uneasy feeling didn't fade. Rubbing her wrists, she sat up.

"Come here." Hunter reached up and drew her down beside him on the bed. With her back pressed against him, his mouth at her ear, he asked, "Was that too much for you?"

"No. It wasn't," she said truthfully. Being tied up hadn't frightened her, not the way she thought it would. It was how much she wanted this man that scared her. "I loved it."

They lay quietly, until his breath tickled her ear and he asked, "What about me, Maggie? How do you feel about me?"

Maggie frowned. "What do you mean?" she asked, rolling onto her back.

He propped himself up on his elbow and looked down at her. "I've fallen for you. Hard," he admitted with a soft smile. "I don't want this to end."

"The sex?"

"That, too. But we're more than that." She felt his chest expand and press against her side as he drew a deep breath. "I'm ready, Maggie. Today I realized that love could be a give-and-take. I've been keeping commitment at arm's length because I felt I was all tapped out. I couldn't provide for my sister *and* the woman I loved."

"Love," she repeated. Her fingers dug into the comforter. How had this happened? This was supposed to be about sex and fantasies, not feelings.

He nodded. "I'm ready, Maggie."

"I'm not," she whispered.

She watched his smile fade.

"The idea of falling in love…it scares me," she continued. "It always has. To give another person that kind of power over my life is terrifying. I've worked too hard to gain control of my life. I don't want to go back to being helpless."

"You don't trust me," he said flatly.

"I do," she said quickly.

He raised an eyebrow.

"But not with my heart." She looked away. "I'm sorry."

He reached down with his left hand and brushed away a few strands of hair. "Honey, I'm not going anywhere. I'll be here when you are. For right now, let's sleep. You have a big day ahead of you tomorrow."

She nodded, rolling back onto her side. Hunter wrapped himself around her, his entire body pressed against hers and his arm slung over her waist. He was so close, she could feel when his breathing changed and she knew he'd fallen asleep.

But Maggie lay awake wondering, thinking. Would she ever be ready to give up her heart? It was risky. What if it didn't work out? Living with her father, she'd always been waiting for the other shoe to drop. And now, with Hunter, she had the same feeling. If she let go, if she fell for him, she couldn't shake the feeling that her world would fall apart.

17

IN THE MORNING, Hunter drove a quiet Maggie to Fort Campbell. He'd gone out first thing, before she woke, to pick up coffee and cinnamon rolls. She'd thanked him, but stopped short of saying the words he wanted to hear: *I've fallen for you, too. I'm ready to set my issues aside and do whatever it takes to make this work.*

But he wasn't raising the white flag yet. He couldn't blame her for not trusting him entirely, not when he'd been holding back from day one, interfering with her book. Maggie's world hinged on her work. If she discovered he'd tried to take that away from her, robbed her of the stable future a tenured position promised, she'd fall apart. He couldn't let that happen, not to the woman he loved.

He'd only known her a week, but a week in his world could be life changing. Hell, the hours he'd spent in Taliban country with a gunshot wound that required a modern hospital had nearly cost him his life. He'd be damned if he was going to ship out again without fighting for Maggie.

Hunter walked out of the office building where he'd just left Maggie with Connor. She had three interviews back-to-back, giving him plenty of time to kill. When he reached the rental car, he opened the driver-side door and slipped inside. He pulled out his phone and dialed. Knowing he was putting his career with the army on the line, he pressed Send. Maggie was more important than his job. He didn't need the excitement of being a Ranger. He'd take a stateside position—from the army or from a private company, whoever was offering—if it meant he could keep Maggie. And after he made this call, after he intentionally disregarded his colonel's orders, he had a feeling the army wouldn't be eager to work with him.

"Hey, Logan. It's Hunter. Yeah, I'm good. Fully recovered. How are you?" Hunter listened to his friend for a minute. He knew his former teammate was still hurting after the loss of his wife to cancer, but he suspected Logan would also understand Hunter's situation. That, and the man owed him. Hunter had never blamed Logan—getting shot was one of the risks of fighting—but he knew his friend held himself responsible.

"Look, man, I've met someone," Hunter said when they'd finished the pleasantries. "And she's it. But I need your help. I need you to drive down to New York for an interview."

MAGGIE GLANCED AT the clock on the wall. She had ten minutes before her third and final interview with Mike, the team medic, the man who'd saved Hunter's life. If anyone could tell her how Hunter had ended up with a bullet in his shoulder, she had a feeling it would be the guy responsible for keeping his injured teammate alive. The other guys had all evaded the question with a "these things happen" answer. But instinct told her there was more to the story. And she wanted to get to the bottom of it, if for no other reason than to keep her mind from drifting back to last night.

Hunter wanted more. Commitment. A relationship. More tie-me-up sex. He'd blown her fantasies away, all right. She'd dreamed about wild, passionate sex and she'd fantasized about a drop-dead sexy man falling in love with her, but to find both with the same man? Not possible— or so she'd thought.

So why hadn't she said yes last night?

Fear.

Maggie pushed back from the table in frustration. She was afraid of what letting an army ranger into her life would do to her, especially one who vied for control. But her fear didn't change the fact that part of her wanted to keep seeing him. Until recently, maintaining control over her life had felt reassuring. But now it felt like an oppressive weight—except when she was with Hunter.

She opened the door to the conference room and walked down the hall to find the coffee machine Hunter had shown her. Maggie smiled at the men and women in uniform sitting in their offices, forcing herself to appear professional, instead of a woman who was wondering what she would say to her potential boyfriend after work.

"How'd your interview go?"

Maggie froze outside the entrance to the kitchen. She recognized Connor's voice. She'd spent two hours talking to him this morning. Only this time, he wasn't talking to her. She shouldn't eavesdrop, but she couldn't resist.

"Great." That voice belonged to Jed, the second teammate she'd met with this morning. "I said what Hunter told me to say."

Maggie tensed. Of course Hunter had prepared his teammates for their interviews. That was his job as her liaison.

"Same here," Connor replied. "But she asked how Hunter got hit. Do you think she'll learn the truth?"

Maggie held her breath.

"Nope. I heard the colonel ordered Hunter to keep a

tight leash on her. Control the message of her book. And if there is anyone who can manage a woman, it's Hunter."

Connor laughed. "You know he spent the last week living with her, right? I mean, he called me from her study in the middle of the night."

"Yeah, I bet he didn't spend the night there. Unless... do you think they did it on her desk?"

Stomach churning, Maggie turned around and stumbled down the hall toward the conference room. She'd heard enough. The coffee she'd had earlier was like acid in her belly. She saw the ladies' room door and immediately pushed her way inside, turning the lock behind her. Hands clutching either side of the white bathroom vanity in the small room, she stared hard at her reflection in the mirror. Her skin was pale and her eyes glistened with tears, threatening to overflow at any moment. The pain was too poignant. Something inside her had shattered, leaving her physically nauseous and emotionally broken.

Her trust.

She had trusted Hunter Cross, and not just in bed. She'd confided in him, giving more of herself to him than she'd ever offered anyone. She'd told him about her childhood and how growing up with her father had left her determined to secure her future. This book was the key. He knew that. And yet, he'd spent the past week trying to manage the message of her work.

Hiding things from her.

While she'd been reveling in the ecstasy she found in his arms and the joy she'd discovered in doing everyday things with him, he had simply been doing his job. The reality felt like a lead weight in the pit of her stomach. She'd known their relationship came with an expiration date. Hunter ran from commitment. He was the wrong man for her, too controlling. And his job? It spelled Disaster—capital *D*.

But what if there had never been a relationship at all? What if he'd been lying to her from the minute he'd walked through the door? All in an attempt to take away the one thing that had helped her through years of living with an unreliable drunk—control.

Maggie looked up into the mirror and saw the tears running down her cheeks. She reached for a paper towel and began wiping them away. She had to get out of here. She couldn't let Hunter, his teammates, anyone, see her like this. They couldn't watch her fall apart over a wounded Ranger who'd said things he didn't mean.

I've fallen for you. Hard. I don't want this to end.

Maggie shook her head, trying to force the words out of her mind. He hadn't meant them. They were simply one more way he could manipulate her. She checked her appearance in the mirror. Not perfect, but it would have to do. She opened the door, determined to keep her head down and her red, puffy eyes hidden. She took two steps and bumped into a solid wall of muscle.

"I'm sorry," she said quickly, trying to step around the man, but he moved with her.

"Professor Barlow?"

Maggie looked up and watched as his smile turned to concern. "I'm Mike. I went to the conference room first, but when I couldn't find you I thought you might have lost your way. Forgive me for saying so, but you look a little upset. Are you okay?"

"No, I'm not. It must be something I ate." Her voice sounded calm and collected, while inside she was falling apart. "If you'll excuse me, I need to be going. I'll call to reschedule."

"Let me walk you out," he said, falling into step beside

her as she headed to the conference room. "I can call Chief Cross for you. He's waiting outside with your rental car."

"No, thank you." She moved around the room, gathering her things and speaking on autopilot, while inside she wanted to curl up in a ball and cry. But she couldn't, not here. It wouldn't be professional. She might pick the wrong men, but she was, above all else, a professional. "I'll call a cab."

But Mike was already on his cell, talking to Hunter. "Hey, man, Professor Barlow's not feeling well."

She couldn't face him. Not right now. Not here in front of his teammates. "I need to leave."

"Ma'am, Hunter will be here in a minute," Mike said, watching her from his post by the door.

Maggie stuffed her computer into her bag and swung it over her shoulder. "When he gets here, tell him I know about his orders. I know it was all a lie."

18

"WHAT WAS A LIE?" Hunter asked as he rushed in, breathing heavily from his all-out sprint to the conference room. His only thought was that Maggie needed him. But the wary look in her eyes told him this wasn't a stomachache. Something had happened.

"Maggie?" He stepped toward her, but she moved away, out of his grasp.

"I know about your orders."

Hunter froze. Cold, hard fear gripped him. Practically everyone she believed in had let her down. And now that list included him. "How?"

"It doesn't matter," she said, her voice sharp. But he heard a slight waver as if she might cry at any minute.

How had this happened? His teammates. It had to be them. But she was right. It didn't matter. She was all that mattered to him.

"I need to leave." She moved toward the door, but Hunter stepped into her path.

"Maggie," he pleaded. He'd never begged for anything in his life, but he was ready to fall on his knees now. "Please don't go. Let me explain."

"Why wouldn't you tell me how you got shot?" she demanded. "You were hiding something, weren't you?"

"Yes." He answered without hesitation. Standing a few feet away, Mike let out a curse. "But I'm not hiding it from you now. Not anymore. While you met with Connor and Jed, I made a call to Logan. It was his mistake and he's willing to tell you everything. How he messed up because his head wasn't in the game. Before we deployed, Logan buried his wife. He shouldn't have been on the mission, but he was and he made a mistake. Logan will sit down with you and tell you everything."

Her eyes narrowed. "Why?"

"Because I asked him to. He's driving down to New York now. He'll tell you what went wrong, and it's your decision whether you print it or not. But Maggie? What happened over there doesn't matter. One man made a mistake. It happens. What matters is that this thing between us, it's real. The time we spent together had nothing to do with your book or my orders."

"What were your orders, exactly?"

Hunter ran his hands through his hair. "To make sure your book made the Rangers look good and to steer you away from the sensitive information we'd rather not see in print."

"How?" she demanded.

"I'm a Ranger. I do what I need to do to get the mission done." On its own, set apart from all the reasons he had to do what his CO asked—Sierra, his promotion, his honor as a soldier—it sounded horrible. Maggie wasn't a Tango he needed to eliminate. She was a writer. And the woman he loved.

"That's why you kissed me that first night. On the patio. Why you let me believe you were drunk so I'd let you stay."

"No. I drank so you'd let me crash on your couch. But I kissed you because I couldn't resist you."

Maggie made a sound of disbelief.

"It was your bra strap peeking out whenever your shirt slipped off your shoulder. I remember thinking about how I prefer you braless, and then I had to kiss you. Maggie, every kiss, every touch, it was real. I wanted you then and I want you now." He stepped toward her, reaching out to touch her—her hand, her shoulder. He craved physical contact with this woman who was slipping through his fingers like desert sand. But she moved away, out of his grasp. She reached the door and turned the knob.

"Christ, Maggie," he said, his hand falling helplessly by his side. "I love you."

"Don't you dare use those words," she snapped, holding the door open. "If this is your idea of love, I don't want it."

SIX HOURS LATER, Maggie heard a telltale thump a second before her grandfather's Mercedes lurched toward the right. Jolted out of self-pity, she steered the car off the road and turned the engine off. She got out to inspect the damage. Just as she'd suspected when she heard the familiar noise, the right rear tire was flat. And to make matters worse, the rim was bent. She must have hit something. Glancing behind her, she saw a big piece of wood that had probably blown into the street from the woods nearby. It had happened before, only today she'd been too distracted to swerve around the debris.

She turned her attention back to the car. Even if she knew how to change a tire, she had a hunch her poor old car needed more than the spare in her trunk. Maggie pulled her cell phone out of her pocket and dialed the one person she could count on to help her.

"You were right," she said when Olivia answered. "I should have picked up a mechanic at the car show."

"What happened?"

"I blew a tire and bent the rim. I need you to come get me. I'm on the road to my house, about four miles away from the bridge," she said, fighting back tears. She'd made it to the airport, through the flight back and halfway home without crying. She refused to break down on the side of the road.

"What else?" Olivia said gently. "I know you're crying, Maggie."

"It wasn't real, Liv," she sobbed. So much for maintaining her composure.

"We're talking about your Ranger now, not the car, right?"

"He was just following orders," she said, struggling to steady her breathing. This wasn't like her. She didn't lose control of her emotions. She didn't feel this deeply. Not for anyone. And it could only mean one thing.

"Oh, God," she whispered into the phone. "I love him."

"Stay in the car," Olivia ordered. "Lock your door. And don't do anything stupid. I'll be there in five minutes."

Eyes wide, her breath coming in sharp gasps, Maggie stumbled back to the car and sank into the driver's seat.

Love.

She leaned her head against the steering wheel as hot tears ran down her cheeks and soaked her fingers.

Oh, God. Oh, hell.

That shattered feeling inside? It wasn't just her trust. She'd gone and fallen in love with the man. Head over heels. And she hadn't even realized it until now.

She'd thought giving her heart would be a conscious choice, something she planned and organized before she said the words, as she had with Derrick. But that hadn't been love. Not real emotional-whirlwind-inducing love, not like this. This was everything she'd always feared. It threatened to rip her to shreds, leaving her world in chaos.

Maggie squeezed her eyes closed against the onslaught of tears. What an idiot. How could she think she had any control over love? She should have known better. After years spent loving a father who'd chosen alcohol over her, she should have realized love wasn't under her control. Love happened. Plain and simple. And it had happened to her.

MAGGIE SAT ON the floor of Olivia's living room surrounded by stick-to-your-thighs calories. Linguine Alfredo. Mozzarella sticks. Chocolate cake. Take-out containers surrounded her, waiting to offer comfort, but her body, her stomach in particular, insisted on wallowing in misery.

"What about lemon cream cake?" Olivia asked, pulling a brown box from the bag. "I ordered all your favorites."

Maggie took the container and set it down beside the rest. "I'm not hungry."

"Not even for cake?" Her friend plopped down on the floor beside her, not questioning why Maggie had chosen the worn blue carpet over the furniture. "Are you sure?"

Maggie shook her head. Beside the Alfredo, her cell phone vibrated. She didn't have to look at the caller ID to know it was Hunter. He'd been calling for the past hour. Part of her wanted to answer just to hear his voice. But another part of her wanted to yell at him for playing with her emotions.

"I can't believe I fell for him. I knew from the start that he only wanted to interfere with my work, but a few kisses, an offer of kinky sex, and here I am."

"You really think he slept with you to stop your questions?" Olivia picked up a fork and dug into the steaming hot container of shrimp scampi. "Seems like an awful lot of effort when he could have simply refused to talk. The man made you s'mores. If he really wanted to mess with your book, I'm sure a person with his training could have found another way."

"My study," Maggie said, a renewed sense of panic washing over her. Oh, God, what else had he done? "After Frida's, I couldn't find him, and then I ran into him near my study. He was probably messing with my computer."

"Well, did he?"

The phone started dancing again, begging to be answered. Maggie pushed it farther away. She was definitely too angry to talk to him. "No, my blog launched on time and there were no changes to my rough draft."

"Have you stopped to think that it might not be so black and white?" Olivia asked. "Maybe what started as following orders turned into something real?"

No, she hadn't. She lived her world in black and white, leaving the murky area in between to people who hadn't had their hearts broken time after time growing up. "But how can I trust him now?"

Olivia shrugged. "Love is risky."

Maggie shook her head. "I grew up surrounded by risk. I've had enough."

"You can't hide behind your past forever. You need to find your future and figure out who you are."

"Who I am? If this book succeeds, I'm a bestselling author and tenured professor."

Olivia stabbed another shrimp with her fork. "Is that all you want for yourself? You went to the car show for a reason, Maggie."

"Because you made me."

Olivia shook her head. "I pushed a little, but you wanted

to go. You might not have realized it then, but you were looking for something."

"Orgasms."

"Is that all?"

Maggie closed her eyes and leaned her head back against the ottoman. "No, I was looking for a part of myself, the part that was buried beneath responsibility and my need to micromanage my life."

"Did you find it?"

Maggie opened her eyes. "Yes." In bed with Hunter she'd found her passionate side. But he'd given her more than fantasy sex. He'd been the person she confided in. He'd taken care of *her* for a change, cooking for her, protecting her from her colleague's wandering hands, fixing her gutters.

"I want what I had this week. The fantasy," she murmured. "And not just the sex. I want the loving, trusting relationship."

"Maggie, if he loves you and you love him, it doesn't have to be a fantasy."

Then why did it still seem so far out of reach? Maggie sighed. "Letting Hunter into my life—trusting him, loving him—means putting my heart out there, and what happens after that? I wouldn't have control of that and it scares me. Liv, what if it doesn't work?"

"Then it ends and you'll hurt," Olivia said bluntly. "But what if you never give him a shot, Maggs? You deserve a little happy in your life, and I think he makes you pretty damn happy. Right?"

Maggie bit her lip. It had been so long since she'd thought about what made her happy. She'd been so focused on taking care of her father and then on her career that she pushed happiness to the side. "When I'm with him, I no longer feel as if I'm hiding part of myself. I can have my career and my, er, cake."

"Is that what we're calling it now?"

"It was supposed to be just one night of amazing sex. How did it get so complicated?"

"It's never just sex. You're not a robot, Maggie. You're a woman who happens to enjoy sex with this man, and you have a successful career. You can have both, but no one said it was going to be easy."

"What if he never wanted me? Not really," she said, voicing the fear that had wrapped around her like a vise when she'd overheard Connor and Jed talking. "What if he was only with me to do his job?"

"Do you really believe that?"

I'm never going to get enough of you. His words from the night she'd made his fantasy come true echoed in her head. That moment, when they'd made love, it had felt sincere. But there wasn't a cold, hard fact she could point to that said, *yes, he meant every word.* She had to take it on faith.

"Maybe parts of it were real," Maggie admitted. Her phone started vibrating again. Maggie leaned over and saw Hunter's name.

"The parts that matter?" Olivia asked.

The connection between them that they'd tried to ignore, but couldn't? She hadn't imagined that, and she knew Hunter had felt it, too. She'd known she was safe to explore her fantasies with him.

And his kindness. That had been real, too. He hadn't repaired her gutters and made s'mores for her because he'd been following orders. For the first time in as long as she could remember, she'd let someone help her, take care of her. And it had felt good.

Maggie nodded. "What do I do now?"

Olivia lowered her fork. "You start by answering your phone before I throw it out the window."

Maggie picked up her cell, which was vibrating again. "Hunter?"

"Where are you?" He sounded breathless, as if he'd been running.

The sound of his voice stirred up her emotions. Desire, love and fear intermingled. Was she making the right choice? Was he worth the risk? "I'm at Olivia's."

"Give me the address. I'll be right there."

"You're in New York?" she said, surprised. "How?"

"You didn't think I'd let you go without a fight, did you? I hopped a military flight." She heard the sound of a car engine turning over in the background. "Now give me the address. I found Logan waiting on your doorstep. He dropped everything when I asked him to meet with you. I'm bringing him with me now, so be ready with your questions, Miss Maggie."

Maggie rattled off the address and then set the phone down, her hands trembling. "He's coming here. And he has Logan with him, his teammate the army didn't want me to interview. He really did it, Olivia. He put his job on the line for me. He loves being a Ranger. More than anything."

"Maybe he loves you more," Olivia said.

"Oh, God, maybe he does." Maggie waited for the weight of this revelation to sink in and threaten to smother her. But it didn't. Instead she felt the first inkling of hope pulling her out of the shattering despair she'd carried around with her since she overheard his teammates talking. If he was willing to put his career on the line for her, his feelings must be real. "What do I do now?"

"You decide whether he's worth the risk. Whether

you believe in him and trust him. Whether you love him enough." Olivia handed her the chocolate cake container. "Here. Eat the cake. It will help you think."

19

HUNTER PULLED UP in front of Olivia's modest one-story cottage. He got out of his rental car and rushed to the front door without waiting for Logan. He had to see Maggie. He needed to know she was all right. And then he had to convince her that his future was here with her.

He knocked, and Maggie opened the door as if she'd been waiting on the other side. He could feel the tension in her body without touching her. She'd changed out of her business clothes into her exercise pants and gray hooded sweatshirt, the one that hugged her breasts. His gaze dropped briefly to her chest before he looked back at her face. She had a smear of chocolate on the side of her mouth. His hand itched to reach out and wipe it away. But he couldn't. Not until he said what he came to say. Not until he was certain she wouldn't pull back and slam the door in his face.

"What happened to your Mercedes? It's not parked out front." He grimaced as he said the words. He should have started with *I love you,* not *where is your car?* But what if something had happened to her? An accident?

"Flat tire," she said. "The rim was bent out of shape. Olivia picked me up and I called a tow truck."

"Next time, call me," he said. "I'll fix it for you."

She stared at him for a long time, as if she was trying to gauge his honesty.

"I mean it, Maggie," he said softly. "If you call, I'll be there for you. Always."

"Maybe I will," she said. She stepped back and held the door open. He watched her fingers drumming against the wooden door. "Would you like to come in?"

Logan, who'd followed him out of the car, said, "I'll wait out here."

"No, please join us." Olivia appeared in the doorway behind Maggie. "You must be Logan. I'm Olivia." She extended her hand, effectively drawing Hunter's reluctant teammate into the house. "Maggie and I went a little crazy with the takeout. Why don't you join me in the living room for a late dinner? You must be starving."

Logan nodded as he stepped into the house. "Yes, ma'am."

"Can I talk to you before you interview him?" Hunter asked Maggie as she closed the door behind them.

She nodded. "The interviews can wait."

For the first time since Mike had called him at the base that morning, Hunter felt some of the tension ease. It was like the feeling he had when he came home from a mission—relief, but uncertain what came next.

"Come with me," Maggie said. She led him down the hall to a small kitchen decorated with the same wild colors Olivia favored when it came to her clothes.

She turned to face him, her arms crossed tightly around her torso. "You risked your career for me."

He heard the disbelief in her voice as if she were waiting for him to correct her. "I did."

Her brow furrowed. "Why? You've worked so hard—"

"I'm not giving up on us," Hunter said, his hands on

his hips. "I'll do whatever it takes. You come first, Maggie." He watched her jaw fall open, her eyes widen, and he realized she'd been a child the last time anyone had made her a top priority. Maggie didn't just need to hear the words "I love you"; she needed to know he wasn't offering an empty promise.

"You mean more to me than my job," he continued. "I've already spoken to the colonel. He knows you're meeting with Logan, and what you choose to print is your call. I trust you to use your judgment and he's going to have to live with that. He also knows I'm leaving. It wouldn't be right to stay after I disregarded his orders, even if it was unofficial. I'm taking a job with a private security company."

Her arms fell and she took a step toward him. Not within arm's reach, but close. "No," she protested. "You love being a Ranger. You can't leave."

"It's done, Maggie," he said. "If you'd asked me last week, I would have told you I couldn't imagine a future where I wasn't shipping out with my team. But now? I'm not sure what I'll be doing for this new company, but I don't think they'll park me behind a desk. And as long as I come home to you, I'm happy. I want you, Maggie. In my bed at night and when I wake up in the morning."

"You meant it when you said you love me."

The hint of surprise in her voice was crushing. His hands formed tight fists at his sides. The fact that she'd doubted his sincerity for even a moment confirmed he'd made the right choice. His job should never come before love.

"I do," he said. "And I'm going to work damn hard to make sure I never give you a reason to doubt me again."

Silence filled the room. He watched as her chin dropped to her chest and she closed her eyes. Oh, hell, had he pushed too hard? Maybe he should have let her talk to Logan first. Maybe she needed more time.

"My turn?" she asked quietly, her voice rough with emotion.

He nodded. "I'm listening."

She opened her eyes and lifted her gaze to meet his. He saw tears threatening and wanted to reach out and wrap her in his arms. But he needed to hear what she had to say. Would she send him away? Call him a liar? Had he broken her trust beyond repair?

She drew a deep breath, blinking back the tears. "I'm ready to take that risk," she said, her voice steady.

Hunter felt as if the weight of the world had been lifted from his shoulders. He took a step toward her.

"But," she continued.

He stopped dead in his tracks. God help him, there was a but.

"I'm scared, Hunter," she said. "Scared it won't work. Afraid you'll break my heart."

"Maggie, we'll make it work."

"Let me finish." She closed the distance between them and rested her hands on his chest. "I'm willing to take that risk. But in return, I want it all. I want the fantasy. My career and you in my life."

Hunter reached out and drew her to him, wrapping her in a tight embrace. He closed his eyes tightly. He hadn't realized until he'd pulled her against him how close he'd been to falling apart, how close he'd come to spilling tears.

"You can have it all," he whispered in her ear. "Miss Maggie, I'm going to do my best to make your dreams come true. And my best is pretty damn good. I might be leaving the army, but I'm still a Ranger. I've been trained to never give up. Ever. I'm going to make you happy. You have my word."

"That's good." She pulled back, but he refused to let her go. She looked up at him, smiling. And he grinned like a fool back down at her.

"Because I'm falling in love with you," she said. "Head over heels."

Epilogue

Five Months Later

MAGGIE OPENED THE cover of the book in front of her and looked up at the young woman standing across the table. "Who should I sign this to?"

"Matt, my husband. He's a marine," the woman said proudly. She wore a white sweatshirt with a sequined American flag across the front. Perfect for the poorly heated indoor event space at the fairgrounds. "He's deployed right now, but should be home for the holidays."

"That's wonderful," Maggie said with a smile. She turned to the title page and signed her name.

"I've already read your book," the woman gushed. "I loved how you made the Rangers seem heroic and human at the same time. A lot of writers would make a big deal out of that one poor man's mistake, but when I read about his wife dying from cancer before he deployed, I just wanted to reach out and hug him."

"Thank you," Maggie said sincerely as she handed the book back to her.

"I plan to give this copy to my husband for Christmas." The woman took her signed book and held it to her chest.

"Thanks for being here. Most military authors stick to the large bases and major cities for their tours."

"You're welcome," she said. "And happy holidays."

The woman walked away and Jane, her publicist, appeared with a stack of books. "Would you mind signing these? There aren't many left. We had an awesome turnout."

"Sure."

Jane plopped her load down on the table and Maggie reached for the first copy. Her publicist took out her BlackBerry and started tapping away. Maggie dropped her pen when Jane let out a high-pitched squeal that sounded more like a junior high cheerleader than a forty-something publishing veteran.

"You hit the list!" Jane announced. "The *New York Times* printed list!"

"Wow. That's great." Shock followed by excitement washed over her. This was her week. First the faculty's review committee had awarded her tenure and now this. Her book had hit the *New York Times* list.

"I need to make a few calls," Jane said. "This is awesome. I hope you have some bubbly on ice at home."

"I do," Maggie said as Jane pressed her cell to her ear and walked off. But would she have anyone to share it with? She glanced down at her watch, not that it mattered what time it was. Hunter should have been here yesterday. But delays happened, especially in war zones.

"Have somewhere to be?"

Her body tingled at the sound of the familiar voice. It had been over a month since she'd heard it and even longer since she'd seen the soldier standing across the folding table.

"I've heard they have great nachos here," she said, forcing her voice to remain calm despite the excitement brewing inside her. "I want to make sure I get there before the stand closes."

Hunter laughed as he walked around the table. She stood to meet him and he drew her into his arms. Her hands went to his chest, pressed against his uniform. From the look and smell of him, he'd come straight from his mission, hopped on a plane to New York and driven to meet her. But she didn't care if he smelled like he'd been traveling for the past twenty-four hours from God-knew-where. He was safe and home with her.

Every time he went out on one of his missions, she held her breath until he returned, and her heart ached for him. Being with him was scary, but not in the way she'd imagined. His private security job hadn't landed him behind a desk. He was out in war zones doing what he did best—and risking his life. But at the end of the mission, he came home to her. She never doubted that. Over the past few months, the wild, out-of-control love she'd once feared had filled her with joy.

He looked into her eyes and she felt a flutter low in her belly. "You're too late, honey," he said. "They stopped serving nachos months ago."

Maggie rose on her tiptoes and brushed her lips over his. He tightened his hold on her, deepening the kiss until every inch of her was pressed against him, and fully aware of how turned on he was. She broke the kiss and looked up at him, content to remain in his arms. "Then we'll have to settle for plan B."

"And that is?"

"You. Me. And a bed," she said.

"I always knew you were a green-light girl." His hands ran down her back and he boldly cupped her bottom.

"Green light?" She brushed her mouth over his jaw,

feeling the stubble on her lips. It had been days since he'd shaved.

"You've been sending out those come-and-get-me signals since we first met."

She looked up into his devilish brown eyes. "And now that you have me?"

He leaned over, his lips touching her ear. "Let's just say I have my own plan B. And it involves a pair of handcuffs."

* * * * *

REQUEST YOUR FREE BOOKS!
2 FREE NOVELS PLUS 2 FREE GIFTS!

red-hot reads!

No Desire Denied

"In one of my books, this would be a plot point. The characters would have to make a decision. Either they find out and deal with the consequences or they keep thinking about it. I would assume that in your job, it pays to know exactly what you're up against. Right?"

"Close enough."

But *he* wasn't nearly close enough. The heat of his breath burned her lips, but she had to have more. And talking wasn't going to get it for her. If she wanted to seduce Reid, *she* had to make the move.

Finally her arms were around him, her mouth parted beneath his. And she had her answers.

His mouth wasn't soft at all, but open and urgent. His taste was as dark and dangerous as the man. That much she'd guessed. But there was none of the control that he always seemed to coat himself with. None of the reserve. There was only heat and luxurious demand. She was sinking fast to a place where there was nothing but Reid and the glorious sensations only he could give her. She wanted to lose herself in them. Her heart had never raced this fast. Her body had never pulsed so desperately. Even in her wildest fantasies, she'd never conceived of feeling this way. And it still wasn't enough. She needed more. Everything. Him. Digging her fingers into his shoulders, she pulled him closer.

Big mistake.

In some far corner of Reid's mind, the words blinked like a huge neon sign. They'd started sending their message the instant he'd told her they would settle what was happening between them now. He'd gotten out of the car to gain some distance, some perspective. Some resolve. But the brief respite had only seemed to increase the seductive pull Nell had on him.

He'd been a goner the moment he'd stuffed himself back into the front seat.

Long before that.

Oh, her argument had been flawless. Knowing exactly what you were up against was key in his job. Reid heartily wished it was her logic that had made his hands streak into her hair and not the feelings that she'd been arousing in him all day.

For seven years.

The hunger she'd triggered while she'd been talking so logically felt as if it had been buried inside him forever. Then once her lips pressed against his, he forgot everything except that he was finally kissing her. Finally touching her hair. He hadn't imagined how silky the texture would be. One hand remained there, trapped, while the other roamed freely, moving down and over her, memorizing the curves and angles in one possessive stroke.

Pick up NO DESIRE DENIED by Cara Summers, available October 22, 2013, wherever you buy Harlequin® Blaze® books.

HBEXP79776

Recovery...one hot night at a time!

It was the cat's fault. Otherwise
Jameson Cartwright wouldn't have tripped and
ruined not only his knee, but also his newly minted
air force career and the Cartwright family pride.
Now he's lying low and miserable—until the girl he
tormented as a kid comes breezing through his
door, looking fresh and sexy. This time, it's *his* turn
to be exquisitely and thoroughly tortured....

Pick up

Back in Service

by *Isabel Sharpe,*
available October 22, 2013, wherever you buy
Harlequin Blaze books.